OTHER WORKS I
JAPAN

The Budding Tree: *, t Edo*
Aiko K.

Embracing Family
Nobuo Kojima

Realm of the Dead
Uchida Hyakken

The Temple of the Wild Geese and *Bamboo Dolls of Echizen*
Tsutomu Mizukami

The Glass Slipper and Other Stories
Shotaro Yasuoka

The Word Book
Mieko Kanai

Isle of Dreams
Keizo Hino

The Shadow of a Blue Cat
Naoyuki Ii

Originally published in Japanese as *Purensongu* by Kodansha, 1990
Copyright © 1990 by Kazushi Hosaka
Publication authorized by the Author through Le Bureau des Copyrights Français
Translation copyright © 2011 by Paul Warham
First edition, 2011

Library of Congress Cataloging-in-Publication Data

Hosaka, Kazushi.
[Puren songu. English]
Plainsong / Kazushi Hosaka ; Translated by Paul Warham. -- 1st ed.
p. cm.
ISBN 978-1-56478-638-8 (pbk. : alk. paper)
I. Warham, Paul. II. Title.
PL852.O77P8713 2011
895.6'36--dc22
                          2011014806

Partially funded by a grant from the Illinois Arts Council, a state agency,
and by the University of Illinois at Urbana-Champaign

This book has been selected by the Japanese Literature Publishing Project (JLPP),
an initiative of the Agency for Cultural Affairs of Japan

www.dalkeyarchive.com

Cover: design and composition by Danielle Dutton, illustration by Nicholas Motte
Printed on permanent/durable acid-free paper and bound in the United States of America

Plainsong

Kazushi Hosaka

Translated by Paul Warham

Dalkey Archive Press
Champaign - Dublin - London

1

My girlfriend and I had just made the decision to move in together when one day I happened to be in Nakamurabashi on the Seibu Ikebukuro Line for work. I stepped into a real estate office in front of the station and before I knew it I'd agreed to take an apartment they showed me nearby. Then the girl dumped me just before the big day and I ended up moving in by myself.

With two bedrooms as well as a living room, dining room, and kitchen, the apartment was much larger than anywhere I'd lived before. The rent was larger too. For a while I wondered where the extra thirty-five thousand yen was going to come from every month, but it turned out not to be a problem. In fact, I found that I was no longer relying on the loans I'd taken out pretty much constantly in the past, and the balance on my credit card finally started to go down instead of up. The explanation for this strange state of affairs is that I was still suffering the aftereffects of the breakup. No matter who I spent time with (in other words, no matter who I went drinking with), I found boredom creeping over me almost immediately. *What am I doing here? Do I really want to spend my time with this person?* These thoughts nagged at me and soured my mood, and within an hour or so of going out I was standing up to make my excuses and head back home. The money I was saving as a result—thanks to a shrinking bar tab and no money spent on late-night taxis home—more than made up for the extra rent.

I had nothing much to do when I got home except read, which made the fact that I never felt much like reading a bit of a problem. It had been years since I'd owned a television, so watching TV wasn't an option either. I wound up putting some music on the stereo while I did push-ups and sit-ups.

Now that I was living in a bigger place I had no excuse for not starting my long-promised exercise regime. Probably the only reason why I didn't go the whole hog and take up running as well was that it happened to be winter when I moved in. Simply too cold. If I'd happened to move into the neighborhood in, say, late March, then who knows—I might have turned into one of life's seasoned joggers, although the fact that the push-ups and sit-ups routine didn't last much beyond the first three weeks suggests that jogging might have been a short-lived enthusiasm too.

Not that I spent *all* my evenings at home doing push-ups and sit-ups. I must have done something else to fill my time, though I can't remember for the life of me now what it was. People asked me the same question at the time. *So what are you doing with yourself these days, now that you're not coming out drinking anymore?* I got into the habit of telling them that I was staying at home doing sit-ups—and must have told the lie so many times that I eventually convinced myself it was true. I also took to vacuuming and doing the laundry a lot. I went from washing my shirts and sheets once every couple of months to washing them twice a week.

There *was* a little more to my life than this, though—most of it involving cats and horse racing.

Racing was something I'd been interested in for a while. All I had to do was open a form guide and the hours went flying by. It was the perfect way of killing time when I didn't feel up to reading a real book. Cats, though, had played no part in my life, until one turned up suddenly on my doorstep one day.

I'd lived in five different apartments over the years, but until now they'd all been on the second floor. This was the first time I'd lived down on ground level.

I moved into the new place in mid-January, and was doing the vacuuming one day a couple of weeks later when I noticed a small kitten standing by the sliding door and studying me through the open screen.

He was a cute little orange-and-white-striped thing, and he was staring intently in my direction, his head peeking in through the open screen. I looked back at him and our eyes met for a few seconds. Maybe he wants to make friends, I thought. I switched off the vacuum cleaner and crouched down to get a closer look, but as soon as I moved, the kitten whipped his head back through the door and vanished from sight.

I stuck my head out after him and looked around to see if I could find where he'd gone, but there was no sign of him anywhere.

He reappeared a few days later, peeping in through the screen door again and looking up at me with his big round eyes and pointy little ears. I took a deep breath and got up quietly from my chair. Bending down, I started to edge over to where the kitten was standing, making reassuring clucking noises with my tongue as I went. But I hadn't gone more than two or three steps before the kitten pricked back his ears in fright and shot off around the corner.

He came again two days later, and then again two or three days after that. I tried to approach him again, but both times he ran away before I could get close. The next time he came, I decided a change of tactics was in order. I stayed put in my chair and pretended to be absorbed in the racing weekly I'd been reading.

Maybe if I pretended to ignore him he would come into the apartment of his own accord, I thought. But when I looked up from my paper, the cat was nowhere to be seen. Maybe this pretending-to-read-the-paper charade was doomed from the start—this wasn't another human being I was dealing with, after all. But surely even a kitten would realize that I was looking at him if I didn't at least pretend to look the other way. What else was I supposed to do? Luckily, he showed up again three days later.

This time, I got up out of my chair as soon as I saw him and tiptoed over to the porch on the other side of the apartment. Putting on a pair of flip-flops, I made my way around the back of the building to where the cat was standing. I didn't really know what I was going to do if I did manage to get close to him. I just wanted to say hello.

Less than a minute later, there I was. The cat was still peering through the open door into my apartment, but he turned his head toward me when he heard me coming. He looked at me quizzically for a few moments, then darted off and disappeared under the shed in front of the building superintendent's office. I knelt down on the ground in front of the shed and made clucking noises again. But I was wasting my time. When I bent down and looked under the shed, the cat was nowhere to be seen.

Maybe I'd have better luck if I had some food to offer. Dried sardines. Checking to make sure I had enough change in my pockets, I hurried off to the local convenience store to stock up on provisions. But I'd never had an occasion to go shopping for dried sardines before, and finding what I was looking for on the shelves turned out to be harder than I'd expected. I wandered up and down the aisles a few times, then gave up and went over to ask for help. *Excuse me, where do you keep your dried sardines?* The look on the face of the student part-timer behind the counter suggested this was the most preposterous question he had ever been asked. Clearly the words meant nothing to him. I smiled sheepishly and made my way back home.

The next day I found what I was looking for in an old-fashioned little store near the office. I put the sardines aside when I got home and waited for the cat to pay me another visit. Four days later, I was still waiting.

Carrying sardines around in my pocket was going to get me nowhere, though. Instead, I took to leaving a small portion out at night as a peace offering, close to where the cat had peered in at me through the screen door. Maybe this would be enough to lure him back again. The sardines were always gone the next morning, but the cat never showed his face while I was around.

Eventually, our paths crossed again. I was on my way back home from Nakamurabashi station one evening in the middle of March, ten days or so after I started leaving out the good-night sardines, when I caught a glimpse of my little orange-and-white friend as I walked down a narrow street not far from my apartment.

He cut across the road about ten meters ahead of me and ducked into a darkened corner of the building where the trash cans were kept. This must be where he lives, I thought. He looked much more at home here, and there was no sign of the skittishness I'd noticed in him before. This time, he didn't try to run away when I approached.

Our eyes met and we looked guardedly at each other as I took three, four, and then five steps forward. The cat gave me a puzzled look. What *is* this guy up to, he seemed to be thinking. I edged a few feet closer and still the cat didn't move. He fixed me with a quizzical stare, his head cocked pensively to one side.

But my next step was a step too far. Suddenly the cat sprang to his feet and got ready to bolt. Maybe I was encroaching on his territory by coming so close? I stepped back and squatted on my haunches. The cat turned to face me again as I crouched down. Then he sat on the ground in front of me and looked up into my eyes, swishing his tail from side to side.

"Hello. You're a happy little cat, aren't you?" The kitten looked up at me with his ears pinned back. A classic sign of wariness and suspicion—even I knew that much. I stopped talking and looked back at the cat in silence. He cocked his ears forward and stared up at me.

Did this count as communication between us? Who knew? Personally, I was pretty pleased with the way things were going. But what was I supposed to do next? The only thing I could think of was to give him some sardines; unfortunately, I'd left my supplies back in the apartment. After a few moments of indecision I made up my mind to go and fetch them. It wasn't as if I had any other ideas. I spoke to the cat again, more quietly this time.

"I've got some nice fish for you at home. You wait here; I'll be right back."

I seemed to have made myself understood much better this time, and the cat stayed still as I got to my feet and backed away slowly, then turned and ran back to the apartment as fast as I could. But when I returned with the sardines, the cat was nowhere to be found.

All this left me feeling a little agitated. I needed someone to talk to, and I decided to give Yumiko a call. Yumiko and I had been classmates in college, but I hadn't spoken to her now for three years or more. Her number wasn't even in my address book anymore, but luckily I still had the card she'd sent at New Year's, with a rough woodblock print on the front.

I had my reasons for turning to Yumiko for advice. Back in college she'd kept an obese tortoiseshell cat as a pet. I'd never been particularly fond of this fat cat myself, and of course there was no guarantee that she even had it anymore—but something told me that if I wanted to talk cats, Yumiko was the one to call.

She came to the phone with the same curt tone she'd always used with me in the past, but I knew her ways well enough by now not to take offense. Our conversation started the way these conversations always do. Yes, it had been a while; and yes, we were both fine. No, she wasn't married, she said, though she did have a kid. Wow, I thought (and said). Congratulations. And then we got to the subject of cats.

"Maybe you should think about starting a family too," she said when I raised the subject. I ignored her remark and came straight to the point. "He's a little orange-and-white-striped kitten," I said.

"Orange tabbies, they're called. For obvious reasons. Don't tell me you didn't even know that."

I told her how the cat had swished his tail from side to side when I crouched down to talk to him, but this only earned me another rebuke.

"Don't you know anything? Cats don't wag their tails when they're happy. That's dogs. When cats move their tails like that it means they're trying to figure out what to do."

Our relationship had always been like this. I knew nothing about the things Yumiko knew about. Yumiko wasn't too hot on my special subjects either, but most of the time I was the one who ended up listening to Yumiko as she went on about whatever it was.

I enjoyed hearing Yumiko talk about stuff I knew nothing about—and she seemed to be amused by some of my theories too. I seemed to cope with her sarcasm better than most people. Some of the things she said rubbed a lot of people the wrong way, but most of the time I was able to shrug off her outbursts as just a normal part of the conversation.

"You'll have to carry the sardines with you everywhere you go. It's the only way. And even then, you never know. When my cat was a baby he didn't even like sardines. Maybe you should try bonito flakes instead. One good thing about bonito flakes—they come in those handy little packets. Much easier to carry around than sardines. You could even use one as a bookmark if you wanted."

She might have been joking about the bookmark part, but it sounded like a pretty inspired idea to me.

But what if I had the same problem finding bonito flakes as I'd had with the dried sardines? I told her about my aborted mission to the local convenience store.

"I've never bought dried sardines anywhere else in my entire life," Yumiko said.

"Maybe it's just my 7-Eleven that's no good then."

"You weren't looking in the right place, that's all. They all sell cat food these days—7-Eleven, Family Mart, everywhere. I bet you didn't even notice."

That last bit was true enough. She was running circles around me again.

"But I asked the guy who worked there and he didn't know either. He looked at me like I was nuts. Explain that."

It didn't take her long.

"He probably wasn't even Japanese. Probably a student on some study-abroad program from China or Korea. Or if he *was* Japanese, you were just mumbling so much he couldn't catch what you said. He probably couldn't understand a word you were saying!"

Her mind seemed to bounce from one beguiling possibility to the next. I was enchanted by her way of looking at things, so different from my own. Yumiko just went right on talking.

"All I'm saying is that even cats have things they like and things they don't. So maybe the bonito flakes are worth a try, that's all."

"But the stuff I put out always gets eaten," I said, getting back to the dried sardines. I wasn't ready to give in to Yumiko's bonito flake obsession just yet.

"How do you know it's not another cat that's eating it?"

It was no good; she was clearly going to win this point too. She gave me the benefit of a few more of her opinions and then we said goodnight—but not before she'd extracted a promise from me that I would carry a packet of bonito flakes with me as a bookmark for the next few days.

I went out to buy some as soon as I got off the phone. There had been something different about Yumiko tonight, I thought, and as I walked to the store I realized what it was. Her voice had changed. It wasn't a big difference, but her voice was lower now—huskier too, somehow. It was the kind of voice you could depend on.

I still remember the moment vividly. I was walking down the road at the time—I know that much for a fact. It wasn't when I was in the convenience store, and it wasn't after I got back home. I can still remember the exact moment when the thought came to me, just as I happened to look up at a cherry tree by the side of the road and realize that it had come into bud. But where I was standing doesn't really matter. I thought of the past three years and the change they had somehow brought about in Yumiko's voice, and how her style of conversation and her way of thinking about life hadn't changed at all—and it occurred to me that these reflections of mine were themselves a sign of how long Yumiko and I had known one another. And it made me realize that the part of me that was deriving comfort and happiness from these idle thoughts as I walked to the store for bonito flakes hadn't even existed back when I was in my early twenties.

I'll have plenty more to say about my dealings with the cat later on, but for now I want to talk about my other obsession from around this time—an obsession that even today still allows me to date my memories of the period as precisely as a calendar: horse racing.

There comes a time in a single man's life—normally in his late twenties or early thirties—when his weekends suddenly get harder to fill. One by one, his friends get married, settle down, and start spending all their free time with their wives. Reluctant to get in the way, the single guy sees less and less of his old buddies, and time starts to hang heavy on his hands. In my case, just one member of the circle I'd been wasting my weekends with since college was still on his own by this stage—a guy four years older than me named Ishigami.

Now, four or five guys together can easily spend a weekend doing nothing in particular and still have a good time. But it's not so easy when there are just two of you. You need to actually *do* something. I think it was this need to find something to do with our time—it didn't matter much what it was—that was the main reason why Ishigami and I started going to the racetrack so often.

Being a few years older than me, Ishigami was already well into his thirties by this time. There was nothing wrong with his looks— in fact, he was probably better-looking than most of us. He went on a few half-hearted dates a year, and slept with women whenever an opportunity arose—but as I got to know him better, I became convinced that he was one of those men destined to remain single for the rest of their lives. When a good-looking guy like Ishigami doesn't make the effort to find a girlfriend (or never stays with the same girl for more than a few weeks if he does), it's hard to avoid the conclusion that the root of the problem lies somewhere inside. With Ishigami, what it came down to was a complete lack of interest in accumulating possessions of any kind.

Betting on horses isn't like playing the stock market; people don't normally think of it as an investment. It was no surprise that someone like Ishigami preferred horses to stocks and shares. But he wasn't the kind of person to get excited about the idea of high stakes and reckless gambling either—the idea that you could win a million yen on a single race or lose everything in a day meant nothing to him. In my experience, it's the ambitious accumulators of this world who are drawn to that kind of thing. And whatever Ishigami was, he was certainly not ambitious. One look at the way he placed his bets was enough to tell you that.

There are normally twelve races in a day's program. As a rule, Ishigami didn't go in for big bets; he liked to spread his money evenly and apparently at random across the day's races. If he started off with a few wins, he would stake higher amounts later on; if he lost in the morning he would play things safe in the afternoon to make up for it.

This often meant that his overall winnings were nothing to write home about even when he did get lucky. If he had 50,000 yen to bet on the main race of the day, Ishigami would put 20,000 yen on a horse at 30-1; 20,000 on another at 20-1; and then hedge his bets by putting 10,000 on a third horse at 6-1. Even if his third-choice horse came in at 6-1 and netted him 60,000 yen, he still ended up winning just 10,000 yen overall. With some people, you could practically guarantee that they would either hit the jackpot with the 30-1 outsider or lose their entire stake on all three horses. But Ishigami almost never lost on *all* his bets, which meant that with him even gambling could get quite monotonous at times.

I endured my own ups and downs by his side, winning or losing heavily on some days, and making insignificant amounts by hedging my bets on race after race on others. But all I was really doing was killing time, and after a while the races all started to blur into one. Before long I was like Ishigami, betting more or less at random and watching idly as the horses ran past. In spite of this we found ourselves spending more and more of our time together at the races, and we were soon talking about nothing but horses even when we weren't at the track.

I knew one other person in those days who was seriously into horse racing. His name was Mitani.

Horse racing was pretty much the only thing Mitani and I had in common. I didn't even know for sure how old he was. I'd always assumed he was six or seven years older than me, but I never actually bothered to ask. We worked for the same company but in different departments; I suppose we must have known each other vaguely for a while, but the first real conversation I can remember having with him happened over at my desk. We were chatting about something else when out of the blue he asked me if I ever bet on the horses.

"It's all a fix, of course," he said.

The general opinion around the office seemed to be that Mitani was something of a weirdo who was best avoided, but I liked listening to him talk. I couldn't say for sure whether this was because he was a good storyteller, or simply because his worldview (if you could even call it that) was built on such bizarre ideas to begin with. Probably it was a combination of both. Besides, I've always enjoyed the company of oddballs.

"The results are all fixed. There's a team of people working for the Japan Racing Association who come up with all the scripts," he

said. He seemed to take it for granted that I would be interested—
he could probably see from the expression on my face that I was
intrigued.

"You remember that race last week, the Winter Bloom Cup?"

The race had been an eventful one, with the winning combination for the first three horses paying out at odds of 70-1.

"That one was pretty straightforward. You remember the names
of the horses that finished first and second? *Northern Chill* and
Plum Blossom Wings, right? Put the two together, and what do you
get? A flower that *blooms* in *winter*, right? In the *Winter Bloom*
Cup? What a giveaway! At first I thought it was too simple to be
true, but sure enough, I was right. But stuff like that is too easy to
figure out. There won't be any bonuses for the guy who designed
that one."

So now it seemed we were taking the existence of the designers
for granted, and moving on to discuss their incentive schemes. I
liked his style, but what he was saying was almost too straightforward to be really satisfying. Mitani must have felt the same way,
because he now embarked on an explanation of a far more intricate conspiracy.

"What about the Dancing Girl Special—another shocking
result. Remember the two horses that started in Lane 6? *Maple
Boy* and *Bush Clover Pegasus*, right? Well, as soon as I saw that, I
thought: This looks fishy! So I take a closer look, and what's the
name of the horse in Lane 1? *Sunny Butterfly!* The boar, the deer,
and the butterfly! Bush clover, maple, and peony!"

What Mitani was implying was that the names of the horses
were some kind of coded reference to the suits in a traditional

pack of Japanese playing cards. The pack is divided up into twelve suits named after flowers and plants associated with the months of the year, with special trump cards for each suit. The combination Mitani was alluding to (the special cards for the bush clover, maple, and peony suits, featuring pictures of a boar, a deer, and a butterfly respectively) would have made a strong winning hand. I found myself almost convinced, conveniently losing sight for a moment of the essential fact that playing cards and racehorses had nothing whatsoever to do with one another. Then Mitani reminded me of the odds for the winning combination.

"First three horses to finish, Lanes 1 and 6: 110-1," he said.

"So how much did you make?"

Mitani shook his head regretfully and carried on talking.

"That's where I went wrong. I thought it sounded too simple. So I figured maybe the maple and the bush clover in Lane 6 were just there as a tip-off to the butterfly in Lane 1. Then I started thinking about feng shui, and I remembered that Saturday was *Red: Seven* in the old zodiac. And that made me realize maybe I should be thinking about the numbers 1, 4, and 7. You know, like mah-jongg. So I look at Lane 7, and the starting horses there are *Dynamo Gypsy* and *Meine Rose*. A butterfly and a gypsy rose! And the name of the race is the Dancing Girl Special? That's it, I thought."

And so Mitani had thrown away his chance of hitting the jackpot with a 110-1 winning ticket.

"I mean—otherwise, why call it the Dancing Girl Special? It doesn't make any sense. The flower cards on their own aren't enough. It doesn't add up. I tell you, if the designer's not going to keep up his side of the bargain, what chance have the punt-ers got?"

There was something endearing about the earnestness with which Mitani was expounding on all this, given that objectively speaking there was not a shred of evidence for anything he said, and for a while I found myself almost taking him seriously. There's a kind of earnestness that leads people to conclusions that most people would regard as madness, and that's what seemed to have happened to Mitani. At least one thing was for sure, though: he was gambling huge amounts at the races.

When I talked to Ishigami about Mitani's conspiracy theories, he just laughed. "Some people think too much," he said. "It's kind of depressing, if you think about it," he said, with a smile still on his face. In fact it didn't really seem to bother Ishigami much one way or the other.

Some people might have worried that Mitani was risking his sanity by becoming obsessed with secret codes and conspira-cies; others might have objected to his crackpot theories on the grounds that he was failing to treat the races with the respect they deserved. I don't think Ishigami, though, was really interested on either point. In a sense, Mitani was desperate to understand the world and how it worked; Ishigami wasn't concerned with this kind of thing at all. Or maybe I'm overstating things; perhaps what it boiled down to was nothing more significant than the dif-ferences between two people's taste in jokes.

But to get back to my experiences with Ishigami at the race-track. Neither of us had anything against the idea of female company, and we were perfectly capable of turning on the charm when we met someone we liked. So if any girl ever expressed interest in horse racing and wanted to come along to see for herself, we certainly weren't going to turn her down.

But our attitude to the races started to change around this time. We'd originally taken up going to the races because we couldn't think of anything else to do; by now, however, it had become the focal point of our social lives—so that if we did meet a girl who was prepared to spend time with us, it would never have occurred to us to take her anywhere else. This didn't strike either of us as a cause for concern—it was well known that true gamblers kept their gambling and their women separate, but since we didn't think of ourselves as gamblers in any real sense, we didn't see why this rule should apply to us. And I knew what Ishigami's response would be if I said anything about it to him. "If you're going to lose because of some woman, you'd be better off not gambling to begin with."

Our ideal companion was a girl who knew nothing about horse racing—someone who would place her bets in the same haphazard way we did. The last thing we wanted was someone who fussed about things. I even fooled myself into thinking that having a first-timer by my side might bring me another much-needed dose of beginner's luck. My own had run out a long time ago.

There's an area on every racecourse called the paddock. This is where the horses are paraded before spectators about half an hour before the race starts. The idea is to get a good look at the horses immediately before they run; in fact, the paddock is normally the only opportunity you have to get really close to the horses. It was here in the paddock that our dates mused out loud on their impressions of the horses' physiques: the color of their coats, the length of their tails, the expressions on their faces, and so on. If any of the horses happened to be wearing hoods, they would often give their thoughts on the hoods too. "Look at the pretty ribbon in that one's mane," they would say; or "That horse in Lane 3 has a really nice tail." Whatever caught their fancy, really.

At many races there would be at least one gray running. These horses have coats that turn completely white later in their lives, though are more or less gray during their racing lifetimes—basically from the age of three to around seven or so—with patches of white here and there. It's not the most impressive of coats, if you ask me, and certainly nothing like the dark sheen of the black and chestnut-coated horses. But for some reason the grays always seemed to prove the biggest hit with the girls. Keiko was no exception. She had invited herself along for the first time today, apparently for no other reason than that she liked the idea of watching Ishigami and me as we wandered around the course.

"I like that one. His coat is a different color from the others."

"Number 8, you mean?"

"Hmm. I love those patches of white. *Very* dashing."

"They're called grays. He'll be white all over by the time he's 10 or 15."

"Wow, how cool!"

And so it went on. The strange thing was that this was far from being the first gray Keiko had seen that day. In the three races we'd already watched, she must have seen four or five of them already—and yet she was reacting to the gray in front of her now as if its color made it unique. It might have been bright pink the way she was talking about it. People who were visiting the track for the first time often seemed to see things in this way. I convinced myself that unless Keiko was an unusually unlucky person, this otherwise unremarkable horse that had so inexplicably caught her attention was a dead cert. I placed bets on every combination that featured Keiko's gray.

But what made Keiko different from the other girls I'd taken to the races was her reaction when I started to win with the bets I'd placed on her horse. Instead of getting excited like most other people would have, she remained in a world of her own. For Keiko, the results of the races themselves seemed to be the least interesting part of the experience.

"I've never seen such neatly kept grass. Too bad you can't say the same thing for the people."

She followed me to the paddock to see the horses again before the next race. There was a gray running again, but this one didn't seem to appeal to her as much as the one that had brought me such good results the last time around.

"Oh look, there's another one of those grays," she said. And then, catching sight of a nervous horse that kept tossing its head from side to side: "Why does that horse keep moving its head around like that? Maybe he's not in the mood for racing today." This didn't sound like much of a tip. I listened attentively to her mumbled remarks as she watched the horses go by, trying to pick up hints on which horse I should back in the next race. The next thing I knew, she was looking over my shoulder at the racing paper in my hands. "So are these the names of the horses in front of us now," she asked, and started to read the names of the horses. Suddenly she stopped reading and said, "Global Hotpot? What kind of name is that?"

"It's not hotpot; it says Hotspur."

"Oh," she said, laughing out loud. That's it, I thought—I put all my money on Global Hotpot, and won again thanks to Keiko's blasé and totally random tips. But even this second successful result did nothing to rouse Keiko from her lethargy. I don't think it even occurred to her to ask if she could come back again next weekend. I reasoned to myself that this might help keep her beginner's luck alive a little longer, and decided to wait patiently for her to suggest going to the races again.

As for the orange-and-white kitten, I hadn't seen him since the time I encountered him in front of my apartment on my way back from Nakamurabashi station. He seemed to have given up on visiting my apartment again too, but this didn't stop me from looking out for him every time I walked home from the station.

I had never paid this much attention to cats before, and I was amazed to learn for the first time how many there were in my little corner of Nerima. After a while it dawned on me that my area of the Tokyo suburbs was nothing unusual in this respect; I was simply noticing things that had eluded me until now.

There were cats everywhere, even in the most crowded parts of downtown Tokyo. I started to notice them late at night in places like Shinjuku and Shibuya, rummaging among the trash and the piles of leftover food in front of hamburger shacks and bars at closing time, or lurking to some mysterious purpose in the shadowy spaces between apartments and office buildings. Sometimes I watched them as they waited between crowds of drunks on their way home, darting from the shadows to rummage for food among the rubbish before the next gaggle of revelers arrived to send them scurrying for cover again.

Before long, I was noticing every cat I came across, and making a mental note of the color and pattern of its fur. This had never happened to me before. It wasn't that I had become hung up on orange-and-white kittens, particularly—and I certainly wasn't crazy enough to think of searching for that one individual kitten as far away from home as Shinjuku. It was more a question of paying attention to what I saw, and of acknowledging the presence of the cats that flashed across my field of vision for a second and then were gone. For some reason this struck me as an important thing to do.

I think it was about two weeks later when I saw the orange-and-white kitten again. This would make it around the end of March. I can't be absolutely sure of the date—although it would have been the start of spring by this time, I'm pretty sure that the temperature was a fair bit colder than the last time I'd seen the cat. But early spring is a funny time of year, temperature-wise, which makes it easy to get confused when you think back on memories like this. I remember clearly that the cherry blossoms were starting to come out on the trees. I was a few houses away from the cherry tree in front of the apartment building where I had seen the cat the last time. I remember looking up at the tree as I walked, and noticing with a smile that the blossoms had started to open.

That was when I saw the kitten again, crossing the narrow lane in front of me and heading for the cover of the apartment building; in an attempt to attract its attention, I made the same clucking sounds with my tongue that had brought me such a resounding lack of success back in February. I wasn't making much progress. It was a pretty uncouth greeting, but the kitten was older and wiser now. Taking a step—or perhaps just half a step—back from the plastic trash cans, he turned to look in my direction.

The cat stopped what he was doing and stared blankly at me with his adorable round eyes. The world hung suspended, and time seemed to stand still.

The kitten and I stared at each other for several seconds. I was as much at a loss as the cat. I was racking my brain for an idea of what to do next when the cat stepped forward and came to stand directly in front of me.

I suddenly remembered the bonito flakes I'd been carrying with me all this time, and rummaged through my bag for the packet. Startled by my sudden movements, the cat pricked back his ears and pulled his head back in alarm. There was caution and suspicion all over his body again. I stopped still, and the cat seemed to relax a little. I opened the packet of bonito flakes as quietly as I could.

The cat watched me warily, and stepped away when I held out some fish flakes in the palm of my hand. But I could see that his little nose was twitching at the smell of the fish.

"Look—bonito flakes," I said in the friendliest tone of voice I could muster; when the cat still didn't make any move, I held out my hand and scattered the flakes on the ground. His nose sniffing eagerly at the scent of the fish, the cat stretched his neck forward as far as it would go. But he still seemed reluctant to trust me, and wasn't prepared to move any closer. It was only when I stepped away that the cat plucked up the courage to venture where the fish flakes lay scattered on the ground. Watching me carefully out of the corner of his eye, the cat started to eat.

The flakes were gone in no time. The cat stepped back and looked up at me expectantly. I scattered some more flakes in the same spot and stepped away. The cat approached the flakes warily and ate these as well, keeping a close eye on me all the time. Then the cat stepped back to his original place, and I scattered some more flakes on the ground.

I tried feeding the cat from my hand again, but he still wasn't interested, and only ate flakes that fell to the ground. The same performance played itself out several times, with me dividing the small bag of flakes into as many tiny portions as possible.

After a while my feet started to feel cold. The season for heavy winter coats was over, and I was wearing only a thin jacket. You feel the cold from your toes up at this time of year—it's a different feeling from the cold you get in the depths of winter. Even so, by the time I had scattered the last of the bonito flakes on the ground, my fingers were numb too.

The cat stepped back when he had finished the final batch and stood looking up at me. By now I was tired of standing out in the cold. "Sorry, all gone," I said. For some reason my voice came out sounding different this time; it wasn't quite the soft, friendly tone I'd used before. I was wondering whether I should try saying it again when the kitten suddenly turned tail and vanished behind the trash cans.

I think it must have been the day after this that Akira came over to my apartment for the first time.

Among my friends was a group of guys now in their late twenties and early thirties who had started making arty and decidedly unpopular independent films back in high school or college. Many of them were still at it now, with or without a financial sponsor. Akira was just 21 or so, and had been hanging about on the fringes of this group for some time, to little purpose. In many ways still a child, he didn't like to talk about his background much. The only thing he'd ever told me about his past was that he had never made it beyond junior high.

His knowledge of the world was certainly limited—he was the kind of person who struggled to read the titles on imported rock LPs—but he was not without his abilities. He was always sending in photos to competitions run by *Young Jump* and other manga magazines, and often won the top prize. Apparently he had scraped enough together from these submissions to make a kind of living for a while—somehow or other he was always able to stay one step ahead of starvation. I can't say much about this aspect of his life—I'd never seen a collection or exhibit of Akira's photos, and I'm not even sure I'd have known the difference between a good photo and a bad one anyway. I had seen a few examples of his work, though. From time to time, and always for no apparent reason, one of Akira's homemade postcards would appear in my letterbox, usually featuring a self-portrait-style close-up of Akira's face. I didn't know much about him, but I knew enough to suspect that there was something out of the ordinary about him.

He called first to say that he happened to be in Ikebukuro. Would it be all right if he crashed at my place for the night? There was something about Akira that made it seem as though the normal rules of polite behavior no longer applied, and before I'd had time to think I heard myself telling him not to bother. And I wasn't joking—I would definitely have preferred him not to come.

Akira's habit of sending photographs of himself to everyone he knew was typical of his character. He had a forcefulness of personality that made spending more than a few moments in his company a wearying experience. Meeting him in a neutral venue in the daytime was one thing, but the sound of his voice on the phone was enough to convince me that having him come over to see me at home—and at night—would be unbearable. But Akira was used to being brushed off, and he came straight back at me with an offer he must have known I'd find hard to resist.

"I'll pick up a couple of girls on the way, if that's okay."

I felt my resistance weakening.

"All right, then. As long as you really do bring someone," I said. What a sucker.

Two hours later, he still hadn't arrived. Maybe he was out there looking for girls, I thought. The sense of anticipation that had come over me as I waited for this unwanted guest to appear was ridiculous. I was starting to resign myself to the fact that he wasn't going to show up after all when there was a loud knock at the door.

I found Akira standing alone on the doorstep. It had taken him so long to get here because he'd walked all the way from Ikebukuro, he said. He seemed to think nothing of it. Of course, if Akira wanted to spend his evenings wandering the streets of Tokyo alone, that was his affair. But he didn't seem to feel that he owed me any kind of apology. He had kept someone waiting for two hours (me), and had even led that person (me, again) to believe that he was bringing girls along. I'd been sitting here giving him the benefit of the doubt, imagining that he was putting the time to good use looking for a suitable pair of young women to bring with him. Instead he had spent more than two hours trudging through the dark on his own because he didn't have 110 yen for the train fare. And none of this seemed to strike him as worth so much as a sheepish look or a shrug of the shoulders.

"Sorry. I'll take the train next time. Don't get mad at me."

His perfunctory apology out of the way, Akira stepped inside and started to give my apartment the once-over.

"Wow. Not bad. A 2LDK, right? Is that what they call it? What does the L stand for, anyway?"

"You don't need to know."

"But this place is seriously cool. A real 2LDK, huh? Pretty impressive. Just the kitchen on its own is bigger than Nagasaki-san's whole apartment. And his place doesn't get any sunlight. He does get the lights from next door, though. Right through his window, all night long. He has to put newspapers over the glass so he can sleep at night. Pretty funny, huh?"

Nagasaki was another filmmaker and something of a hero figure for Akira. Work came in sporadically, and his finances were perched permanently on the brink of disaster. Nagasaki's lack of funds was a source of endless fascination and amusement for Akira.

"Did you hear about what happened the other day? Nagasaki got hired for this job and the guy who hired him never paid. He was so pissed about it he kicked these rocks on his way home? You didn't hear about it? Seriously? Shit, wait till I tell you this one."

"Maybe you should start by asking if I want to hear it first."

"Whatever. So he kicks these rocks—or at least, what he thinks are rocks. But it turns out to be concrete. One of those things where there's like a big lump of concrete sticking up out of the ground? One of those. So he lashes out at it with his foot, and it rips the leather right off the bottom of his shoe. Lucky he didn't break his foot too, right?

"But what about the size of this room? Wow. Yamamoto-san's place is way smaller than this, and there's two of them living there now since Akemi moved in. He likes to tell everyone he lives in a 2DK, but really it's just one room knocked into two. You go in through the front door, and by the time you've taken ten steps forward you've walked through all three rooms and fallen out the other side. But your place really is two separate rooms—one on the left and one on the right. And I bet this place gets some serious sunlight during the day. This is way better than Yamamoto-san's place. Way better. But how come . . . ?"

Akira finally paused to draw breath. He turned to me with an enigmatic smile and when it became clear that I didn't understand what he was hinting at carried on with his babble of questions.

"How come you moved into such a big place on your own? I mean, you're not getting married right? Wait a minute . . . Holy shit. I know what it is. You were supposed to move in here with some girl and then she dumped you. Is that really true? Oh . . . my . . . God. Well, you've got me for company now. No more lonely nights! I'll make you a tape with some good stuff on it next time I come. Good songs to listen to when you've got a broken heart."

I was struck by the way that people and things were twisted out of shape as they entered Akira's world. Maybe he did have some kind of talent after all.

I managed to shut him up for a little while by sending him into the bath, and then won myself a bit more peace by plying him with whiskey. After a while he went into the bedroom where the stereo system was and proceeded to take my LPs down from the shelves one by one, playing a track or two from each before moving on to the next record. I resigned myself to the inevitable and went into the other room and spread out my bedding there for the night. This seemed to cause Akira to lose all interest in my record collection. Instead he took to coming into my room at five-minute intervals and prodding me till I woke up.

Every time he came in, I'd push him away or make as if to kick him from my futon, but nothing I did could drive him away for long. Eventually the irritation got to be too much, and I raised my fist and threatened to punch him if he didn't cut it out once and for all. Unfortunately, I ended up going further than I had intended. I lashed at him in the dark, and felt my clenched fist make contact with Akira's temple. Evidently I had landed a powerful punch. Akira fell to the ground and lay there moaning in pain. I knew him well enough by now, though, to realize that his mad antics would start up again the moment I went over and showed him any sign of sympathy. I decided to ignore him. After a while, Akira stood up and limped his way into his own room, a thin moan still sounding from his lips. He was up again almost immediately, though. I listened as he walked to the kitchen and set about demolishing a packet of instant noodles.

The next morning I overslept and didn't wake up until a good two hours after I was due at the office, only to find Akira just surfacing too. It was almost as though he'd been waiting for me to get up. We were sitting over coffee when Akira suddenly made an announcement.

"I think I'll stick around for a bit. I've decided I might as well stay here for a few days."

I thought it over, and decided it wasn't worth getting upset about. I'd be out of the apartment most of the day, anyway, and would hardly have to put up with him. I handed him the keys and left for work.

Wherever Akira went, he carried a large canvas bag slung over his shoulder. This bag contained more than just a simple change of clothes. All the clothes he owned were in that bag. He lived by crashing at friends' apartments, a few days at a time. When he announced that he was thinking of stopping by to say hello, we all knew what to expect.

Akira stayed with me for three nights and then moved on to crash somewhere else, only to be replaced by his buddy Shimada, another would-be artist drawn to Tokyo from the provinces by his infatuation with Yada and his unwatchable avant-garde films.

Shimada would have been in his mid-twenties, I guess. In his own way, he was every bit as odd as Akira. Originally from somewhere down in Kyushu, he had spent a year or so in the medical department of some college there before dropping out and enrolling at Hokkaido University instead. That was where he came under the influence of Yada, who had gone up to Sapporo to show one of his 16mm films. Shimada dropped out of college again at the end of his second year in Hokkaido, and when he heard that there was a spare apartment in Yada's dilapidated flophouse of a building, he booked himself a seat on the next plane for Tokyo.

Despite all the time he had spent in Tokyo filmmaking circles since then, Shimada had not produced a single film. This was no surprise to anyone who knew him. He was idleness personified, and seemed to spend most of his time slumped half-asleep in his apartment. I stopped by to see him there one afternoon and found him in bed with a thick test prep workbook propped open in front of him. *Practice Drills for the Professional Standards Examination in the Safe Handling of Fuels, Second Level*, or something like that. You know the kind of thing.

"Hey Shimada, what's up? Studying for a test?" I asked.

Shimada talked in a hurried, stop-and-start barrage of disconnected syllables that always made him sound as if his tongue was too big for his mouth or something.

"No. But there's nothing else to read. I found this when I was back home. The other day. So I picked it up. And brought it back."

This was not the answer I'd been expecting.

"But it's really boring," he said. In spite of this, he went on reading for a while, apparently eager to get to the end of the chapter before setting the book down and talking to me.

His apartment was being used as the location for one of Yada's films, so Shimada came to stay at my place for ten days or so. He seemed to regard this as perfectly natural. After realizing that he wasn't cut out to be a filmmaker, Shimada had held a succession of short-lived odd jobs in *pachinko* parlors and fast-food joints. By this time, though, he'd been at his current job for over a year, and had already risen to manager or supervisor of some kind in a computer software company.

Shimada arrived at my apartment in a suit and tie with a paper bag under his arm. He took off his suit jacket and laid it down on the floor next to the futon, before getting in under the sheets and falling asleep fully dressed. He didn't even bother to take off his tie or pants. He had a change of socks with him in his paper bag, so that all he had to do when he woke up in the morning was slip into a fresh pair of socks and pick up his jacket, and he was out the door.

Shimada was more than just tall and spindly: he didn't have any muscle mass at all. Together with the ghostly paleness of his skin, this made his upper body a pitiful thing to behold. I'd always assumed that stick-people like Shimada didn't sweat as much as average human beings, but it still came as a shock when Shimada didn't show any interest at all when I ran the bath every evening. As a general rule, he headed straight for bed as soon as he came in from work, occasionally pausing to down a glass or two of my whiskey on the way. For a whole week he didn't go near a bath or shower. He didn't even change his shirt, and as far as I could tell he didn't seem to think that there was anything out of the ordinary in his behavior. On the eighth night since arriving at my apartment, when it was almost time for him to move back to

Yada's place, he finally announced that he too might as well have a bath tonight. In honor of the occasion, he even changed his shirt and underwear.

A few minutes later I was treated to the sight of a man just out of his evening bath standing with his chin in the air and struggling to fasten the top button of his shirt. But even Shimada drew the line at putting on his tie before going to bed—at which I felt something that was almost but not quite disappointment. The feeling was one I often have—a sense of something that vanishes into intangibility just before you can grasp it and put it into words. This was true of things in general where Shimada was concerned—things would disintegrate and disappear before you could find the words to describe them. This sense of something nebulous, forever on the point of taking form verbally, but never quite doing so, is one that comes back to me even now from time to time, allowing me to taste again the pleasant sensation I often had back then of drifting aimlessly yet enjoyably through the days. With Shimada, there was none of the forcefulness of personality you felt when you were with Akira—there was a vague sense of something strange and amusing when you were around him, but this communicated itself without ever imposing. His was an oddness that knew how to keep its distance.

The shooting went on a few days longer than planned, and Shimada ended up staying with me for nearly two weeks. Time drifted by so vaguely and purposelessly when he was with me that when I think back on those weeks now I can't remember a single conversation we had. After a while it became almost impossible to distinguish one day from the next. When he did eventually move back out, he took with him volumes 4, 5, and 6 of a ten-volume set of paperbacks I hadn't looked at since the day I bought them.

"You don't mind if I borrow these, do you? Now that I've started . . ." As he left, he added that he would make sure to stop by from time to time to borrow more books and spend a few more nights on my floor.

The tempo of daily life—or whatever you want to call it—had been out of balance since Akira came to stay, and I had neglected my new routine of putting out dried sardines for the cat when I got home. This didn't cause me any great amount of remorse; in fact, I was inclined not to care at all. I was pretty much convinced by now that it wasn't my orange-and-white kitten that was eating the fish flakes after all, but some other cat.

The weather had started to get warmer around the time Shimada came to stay. The cherry blossoms that were coming into bud when Akira was there burst into bloom and then started to fall in cascades from the trees in front of the apartment. As usual, I didn't bother going to any blossom-viewing parties. Even so, I realized that I was taking more pleasure and enjoyment from the blossoms with every year that passed. When I was out for a walk I would go out of my way to choose a route that would take me through parts of the city where I knew there were plenty of cherry trees. Once or twice I even slipped out of the office to spend half an hour or so walking through the thick mass of blossoms at Chidorigafuchi.

It must have been the day after Shimada moved back to his own place that I encountered the little orange-and-white cat again as I was passing by the same apartment building where I had seen him before. The cherry tree at the side of the street was coming into leaf, and there were just a few hardy blossoms left on its branches now. I spotted the cat as he darted out a few meters in front of me, cutting across the path and diving into the area where the plastic trash cans were kept.

We followed the same routine as at our previous meetings, even down to the ridiculous shushing, clicking noises I made with my tongue. For some reason, I was still convinced that these sounds would persuade the cat to give up on the trashcans and turn his attention to me instead. The cat shot straight past me to a bike rack a few meters further into the shadows, where he stopped still and turned toward me, his whole body on high alert and ready to bolt again the instant I made a false move.

The cat poked his head from between a pair of parked bicycles and stood fixed to the spot, looking at me with his ears pinned back. He was obviously still playing hard to get.

I had five small packets of bonito flakes in my bag. My plan had been to sprinkle a trail of fish flakes along the road that would eventually lead the kitten back to my apartment. There was something childish about the idea—but that was part of its appeal. There is nothing like the pleasure to be had from devoting your energies to the serious performance of something frivolous. But my hopes were dashed when I saw how nervous and suspicious the cat continued to be whenever he was around me. Perhaps I'd been too ambitious to think that the cat would accept me as a friend so soon. Naïvely, I'd imagined that our relationship could only get closer as time went by; it occurred to me now that I might drive him away altogether if I tried to get too close too soon.

I opened a packet of bonito flakes as quietly as I could and scattered some of the contents on the ground in front of me. A gust of wind blew half of the flakes away almost immediately. But probably we were too far apart for the scent to carry anyway. We stood and looked at each other in silence. The only thing that moved was an occasional fluttering of blossoms as the last flowers fell from the branches of the cherry tree overhead. I was starting to worry that even this might be enough to startle my little friend into flight, when a single petal landed on a spot immediately in front of the cat's nose.

He pinned his ears back and leaned forward with his head close to the ground and sniffed at the petal. Suddenly, the tension and suspicion in his body seemed to disappear. As I watched the cat sniff at the fallen cherry blossom, the wind that had been swirling around us died down. The blossom was a toy that had fallen like a gift from above at the paws of this little stray. I was only making a nuisance of myself. Leaving the open packet of bonito flakes on the ground, I took my leave and went on my way.

2

When I got home I wanted to talk to someone about what had just happened on the cat front. And who better to listen to what I had to say than Yumiko, my old cat-loving friend who had become a mother without bothering to let me know? I gave her a call. She listened for a while and then interrupted with a question I hadn't seen coming at all.

"Maybe there are two cats that look the same. Had you considered that?"

I'd been so enchanted by the image of the little kitten as he leant forward to sniff at the fallen cherry blossom that I'd pushed aside my doubts about his unexpected reaction.

"That's what you said before too. Always thinking outside the box, huh?"

The last time we'd spoken, she'd pointed out that just because the food I left kept disappearing didn't mean my little kitten was visiting me. There might be another hungry cat in the neighborhood. Whether she remembered this I have no idea; it didn't really matter to either of us whether she did or not. Yumiko continued in a nonchalant tone.

"That's just the way cats are," she said. "You're not a real cat-lover, are you, really? Not yet."

Ever since we were just twenty years old, she'd had a talent for giving voice to doubts I'd been harboring at the back of my mind. I didn't bother arguing; she was probably right.

"One thing I have learned: There are stray cats everywhere. I've seen them wandering around places like Shinjuku and Ikebukuro late at night."

"I bet you didn't even notice that until recently. People who don't really like cats don't see them at all. So maybe you are making progress. Cats don't show themselves to people who can't see them. It's only since you learned to take notice of cats that you have started to exist from their point of view. You're still a novice.

"You need to be more humble with them. I bet you're not even putting out the dried fish anymore. The thing with cats is this: you can't just choose one of them. Cats are a totality—it's all or nothing." From anyone else, this would have sounded metaphorical, symbolic—but I knew that Yumiko meant it literally.

I decided to take everything she said at face value. We chatted about other things for a while and as the conversation came to an end I promised that I would start putting food out in front of the apartment again. As soon as I hung up I went to the convenience store and bought eight cans of cat food. I still had several packets of bonito flakes left, but I was no longer sure that bonito flakes were the best thing for my purposes. Perhaps I could make my friendly intentions less ambiguous by putting out official cat food—something that had been made especially with cats in mind.

I pried open the first tin as soon as I got home. An almighty odor stung the back of my nostrils and filled the room. This was going to be way more effective than dried fish. A cat would sniff this stuff out from half a mile away at least. The thought worried me a bit. What if some other cat—a bigger, stronger, and uglier cat—came along and shunted my orange-and-white kitten aside? But then I remembered Yumiko's admonishment. I resolved to embrace the totality of cats everywhere. From now on, I would be friends with all cats, wherever they might be found.

It occurred to me that this new food might prove so alluring that I'd soon find myself swamped with more cats than I could handle. I pictured a mad melee of cats banging heads as they fought to get to the feast in front of my apartment, and imagined the enormous fight that might break out. Once you let your mind start thinking these thoughts, there's no end to it.

The label told me that the tin contained 210g of cat food. I decanted a quarter of the contents into a separate container and left it outside. When I looked the next morning, it was all gone. Probably this should have come as no surprise, since the same thing had always happened with the sardines. Nevertheless, I felt pleased at the outcome and decided to put out another quarter of the can before I left for work. As soon as I got home that evening I rushed over to inspect the tin of cat food. There was no sign that it had been touched at all. The meat was still there where I had left it, slightly discolored and starting to display the first signs of the decay that makes rotten cat food an almost uniquely unlovely thing.

It smelled different now. The food had been out in the sun all day; no wonder it was starting to go off. The area in front of the apartment must be busier during the day than I thought. I threw away the untouched cat food and replaced it with another quarter from the original can. People were probably walking back and forth in front of the building all day. And then there were the neighbors on either side of me, who would be out and about doing their laundry and whatever else it was they got up to while I was at the office. This would certainly make it difficult for a cat to come and eat what I'd put out that morning. I decided that from now on I'd only put food out at night. When I thought of these cats coming to eat the portion I was putting out now, I felt as though the cat food represented a secret message I was exchanging with these cats I couldn't see.

It was less than a week after this that Akira came to stay with me for the second time—just three weeks after his first visit.

Three weeks was an exceptionally short period of time for Akira; normally you went two or three months without hearing from him at all. And when he did finally get in touch after several months of silence, he started talking as if you'd seen each other just a day or two before. As soon as I heard his voice I knew he was worked up about something.

"Home alone again tonight, huh? What's up—you not going out drinking so much these days? We must have some kind of special connection. Anyway, I'm at Nakamurabashi station. You don't mind if I come over?"

Akira was going about things in his own way as usual.

"If you bring a couple of girls with you, sure."

He'd obviously been expecting this. "Funny you should say that," Akira said, unleashing an over-the-top laugh like something out of a modernist drama.

"Not two, though—just the one. But she's a real beauty. Worth three normal girls, at least. You'll love her."

"What good is that going to do *me*?"

"Don't worry, you can talk to her all you want. No charge. You're in your thirties now. You should consider it a privilege to talk to a young girl at all. Everyone will be really envious for you."

"Envious *of* me, you mean?"

"See, it's already happening. Ok, we'll be right over. Give us a couple minutes."

The girl he brought with him was Yoko.

Akira shouted through the door when he arrived, and I opened to find Yoko standing a step or two behind him on the doorstep. "Hello," she said, and gave me a lovely beaming smile. Most of the time when someone smiles it doesn't really do their face any favors—they get big cheeks and creases, and the symmetry of the face is thrown out of balance. You know the person is smiling at you, and it's the thought behind the smile that makes the person's face look attractive or cute or pleasing or whatever. But Yoko's face lost none of its balance when she smiled—her features remained neat and well arranged. And cute.

The typical reaction on being presented with such a perfect face would have been to think, "Son of a bitch"—the words being directed at Akira rather than Yoko, naturally. And for a moment these were more or less the sentiments that did cross my mind. I'd always considered it impossible that any girl from a normal background would ever date someone like Akira.

Akira took hold of Yoko's hand and stepped briskly into the apartment. His attitude seemed to go beyond a sense of brazen entitlement—rather, there was an innocence about everything he did. He looked the place over again and said: "Just the place, don't you think?"

Yoko sounded almost surprised at first. "What, you mean we're staying the night?" But the surprise didn't last long. "Oh yeah, I forgot. The trains will stop running soon." The two of them talked the situation over as if it had nothing to do with me at all.

Yoko started toward a chair in the kitchen, but changed her mind halfway and went over to look out of the window. Her attitude was subtly different from Akira's—to look at Yoko standing there by the window, you'd have thought she'd never lived anywhere else in her life.

I was surprisingly affected by this attitude, at least partly because of the unusually natural smile she'd given me as she stepped up into the apartment. I was musing about such things as I watched her by the window when Akira whispered in my ear that he had picked her up three days ago in Yoyogi Park. This was enough to convince me that Yoko—like Akira—had not a penny to her name, and no job or college classes to attend either. Fate had brought her together with Akira, whose perpetual lack of money seemed to cause him no concern whatsoever. Yoko turned back from the window to ask me a question.

"You don't have any fields out here, then?"

"Just because you're out in the suburbs doesn't mean you're going to be surrounded by fields, you know."

"But we definitely saw fields on the way."

"You can see a few from the apartments upstairs, if that helps. Just beyond the neighbor's place."

"Doesn't the smell of manure ever bother you?"

The idea seemed to delight Akira.

"Does it?" he said. "You can really smell manure from the fields? I never thought of your place as in the country before. But come to think of it, maybe it is. Wild. Yeah, this probably does count as the countryside already. I mean, you have to change trains at Shibuya or Shinjuku to get here. And let's face it, there's no way you could afford to live in an apartment like this if it wasn't out in the middle of nowhere."

"Just think, there are places with fields that you can get to in just one train ride from Shinjuku or Shibuya," Yoko said. "Even Tokyo is like the countryside if you think of it that way."

It was hard to tell whether Yoko wanted to see the fields or not, whether the idea of Tokyo being like the countryside was one that she found enchanting or unspeakably tedious. I wanted to ask her what she really thought, but I knew that my question was likely to come out sounding awkward and dumb. I asked it anyway. "And what do you think about that, about Tokyo being like the country-side?" "Oh, nothing much," she said. "The breeze is nice. Even at night," she said, and turned back to gaze out of the window.

After a while Akira said he was going to have a bath, and asked Yoko if she wanted to join him. She didn't. Maybe she was embarrassed at the idea while I was around. Or maybe she didn't want to share a bath with him in the first place. Anyway, they ended up bathing separately; after their baths Akira suggested that she sleep with him in the room next to mine. She had no objections to this idea. The force of Akira's presence had been almost overwhelming when he'd barged in on my solitary life the first time, but even

Akira behaved a little differently now that there was a girl around. I saw no reason to change my daily routine, and I went out to put another quarter of a can of cat food in the empty can outside just as I had the night before.

The next morning Akira announced that he'd decided to stay for two or three more days. Apparently Yoko would be staying too. Was this a sign that things had clicked between them overnight? Or was it just that Yoko wasn't a girl to make a fuss about her sleeping arrangements? I had no idea. I handed Akira the key as I left the apartment. I was just telling him to pop it in the letterbox if he needed to go out when Yoko spoke up from her position by the window.

"That empty can. Outside. What's it for?"

I didn't feel like explaining the real reason (what was the point?), so I told her it was a good-luck charm.

"A good-luck charm for what?" she asked. The idea of empty cans of cat food with magic protective properties didn't seem to strike her as odd. I was stuck for an answer at first, but by the time I'd put on my sneakers I knew what I was going to say.

"Communication with invisible creatures."

I didn't know myself whether this was the truth or a lie. I stood up and went off to work.

Not long after I arrived at the office, Mitani came over and asked if I was free to talk. Given the fact that he was already standing there talking to me, he must have assumed before he came over that time would be hanging heavy on my hands. He wasn't wrong at all. I left what I was doing and went with him for a coffee around the corner.

As always, we said nothing until we were sitting down.

"So, how you been?"

His voice was weary enough to have convinced anyone who didn't know him that he wasn't in the mood to talk at all. But that was his way; it always took him a while to warm up. Once he got going he told me with mounting excitement about his latest foolproof method of winning on the horses.

"Wait till you hear this one. This one's a winner for sure," he said, digging around in his bag and pulling out a chart he'd drawn up with pink and blue and yellow markers.

A course of races consists of four Saturdays and four Sundays: eight days in total. Mitani's chart showed the results of all the races held on the six previous days of the present sequence and (so he claimed) could be used to predict the winning combinations for the two days still to come, based on an analysis of the jockeys and stables that had won so far. Of course none of this had anything to do with any of the other theories Mitani had previously sworn by, but that didn't matter. His methods changed every week. When he wasn't actually at the races, Mitani seemed to spend most of his free time trying to decode the secret messages being sent to him by the Japan Racing Association.

"Look at this here," he said. "Okabe is in Lane 4 for three races on the same day. You didn't notice? He's riding in four races, and in three of them he's in the same lane? Kind of suspicious, don't you think? It came to me suddenly, about halfway through the races last Saturday. I wish I'd have noticed it earlier. After the races were over I ran home and copied out all the results for the previous four days' races. And this is what I got."

Mitani set the chart down on the table in front of me again. So now I knew that Mitani's attempts to crack the racing code weren't confined to weekday evenings after all.

"And then—what do you know?—the same thing happened again on Sunday. Remember Shibata, the master jockey? Only raced five times. And out of those five races, he was in Lane 6 three times. I mean, what are the odds? And look at this one— he only wins once, in the middle race—the least popular race of them all."

The materials Mitani put together to back up his theories got more intricate and complex with every new solution he found. Not that this made them more convincing. If anything, it only served to make his ideas seem wackier than ever. He was undeterred though, of course.

"I was up till three in the morning drawing up all the details, and then when I finished I was so excited I couldn't sleep.

"I mean, think about it: Put ten thousand on, and you'd win eight hundred thousand back, right? So I started making a shopping list—you know, what I was going to spend my money on. New leather jacket, new bag, stuff like that . . .

"And then the girl I'm seeing is kind of high-maintenance. I thought I'd better take her on a trip. I decided to save Hokkaido for the summer—you don't want to go up there in the cold—and I figured somewhere like Izu might be good. So that's around fifty thousand each for two nights—call it a round hundred thousand. It's a lot of money—so I thought maybe I could claim my half as business expenses . . . anyway, before I knew it was six in the morning.

"Then I remembered my loans. I owe half a million. So I figure I'll pay back around two hundred thousand of that out of my eight hundred thousand, and then . . ."

So how had it gone? Had he actually won the money, or had he slept in and missed the races altogether?

"Sleep in? Are you kidding? This is serious. Whatever happens, I'm going to keeping putting my money on till the scheme comes good. This is like a live experiment.

"Anyway, in the sixth race Okabe was a dead cert, just like I thought. So far, so good. But the other guy I'm not so sure about. I figured none of the guys from Hieda Satoshi's stable were going to really go for it. Still too early. So I held back on that."

There were twelve races in a day, but (according to Mitani) only in three or four of these were all the horses and their jockeys really serious about trying to win. In the other races, no matter how many horses were officially entered in the race, only three or four of them were for real; all you had to do was figure out which they were, and you were home and dry. This is what Mitani meant when he referred to a horse "going for it." But however you sliced it, the result was the same: Mitani's new scheme had failed to bring home the goods. Not that this indicated any problem with his method, of course—the chart I was looking at now represented a fine-tuned, perfected version of his hypothesis.

"They change the way they do it with every meeting, though. People would figure things out if they used the same system two meets running. They never do the same thing twice.

"But it doesn't matter. This weekend, I guarantee results. We haven't had the jackpot race yet. They'll give it to us this weekend—either Saturday or Sunday, you mark my words."

"They," of course, were the Japan Racing Association, although most people would not have thought of a winning bet as something that was "given out" by the organizing authorities. For Mitani, though, who saw the whole thing as a fascinatingly elaborate fix, there was no other explanation.

"And I'm going to get it!" He was almost shouting now. "This is the big one. I'm going to put 30,000 yen on. That's three million if you hit the jackpot. Three million." He was quiet for a few moments and spoke again in his normal voice. "See you around," he said and got up to leave. When Friday afternoon came around and the racing paper came out with the details of the weekend's races, I saw that not one jockey would be riding in the same lane for three races. Mitani would have to work out a new theory, and I couldn't help wondering what it would be. He was sure to come up with something, and the anticipation of hearing his latest schemes made me look forward to seeing him again the following week.

I got home from work a little earlier than usual that night to find that Yoko had worked out the significance of the empty can of cat food. It didn't take much intuition on her part, given that there were three or four cans of cat food in a corner of the kitchen and another half-empty can in the fridge.

It was Akira who told me the news. Apparently Yoko had made her breakthrough around lunchtime, Akira told me in hushed tones as soon as I got home. She had skipped over to the fridge and put the left-over cat food in the empty can outside, and had been waiting by the window ever since for the cat to come and eat.

It soon became clear that what Akira really wanted to talk about was not the fact that Yoko had found out about the cat, but the consequences that this discovery might have for him.

He seemed to be worried that Yoko might transfer her affections to me.

"But it's not me she likes—it's cats," I said. But this wasn't the answer Akira wanted.

"Comes to the same thing," he said. "What am I supposed to do if she starts liking cats more than me?"

So he was now comparing himself to cats, and worrying that he was going to come off second best. Talk about the power of love.

"I'm sure she's always liked cats. You'll just have to try to come between them. Good luck," I said, giving him neither advice nor encouragement.

"But if you like cats, and she likes cats . . . then that gives you something in common, right? So you guys will have all this stuff to talk about, and I'll get left out," he said.

"Well, if that's the way you feel, maybe you should try to become a cat-lover too."

"Come on, that's not how it works." I suppose it was my fault that the conversation wasn't going anywhere, since I wasn't interested in giving him any serious advice. We batted words at each other for a while until Yoko came over. "I've been watching from the window ever since it got dark, and not a single cat has turned up. You do put cat food in that can outside, right?" Cats seemed to be the only subject on her mind.

"What kind of a cat is it?" she asked. This was not looking good for Akira.

"I don't know," I said.

"But you're feeding it, right?"

"Yeah, but only recently. And only at night. It comes and eats during the night, so I never see it."

"And the food's always gone the next morning?"

"Apparently."

"So all I have to do is stay up all night and wait for it to come?"

This, I knew, was going to mean that Akira would be kept waiting as long as Yoko was awake. I glanced over to see his reaction; he caught my eye and shot me a look of theatrical distress. He can't be that upset, I thought, if he can still put on an act like that. I decided to take a chance.

"I'm sure Akira will help you. He'd do anything for you, Yoko, even if it meant taking turns to stay up and keep watch for the cat. Right, Akira?"

Akira didn't have time to say anything before Yoko jumped at the suggestion.

"You will? You'll stay up with me?"

He had no choice but to mumble his agreement. I knew that Akira would be so desperate to spend just one minute more looking at Yoko's beautiful face that he would not be able to sleep while it was her turn to stand guard.

I knew from personal experience that when you were really crazy about a girl, you'd happily go even three nights without sleep so long as you could be by her side. In fact, this only seemed to make you like the girl even more. Of course, there was no guarantee that the girl wouldn't find this kind of behavior annoying after a while; it depended on the girl, though, and I had a feeling Yoko wasn't the kind to worry too much about that kind of thing. I'd only been joking around, but now it looked like Akira was going to be put out a bit. But I wasn't particularly concerned.

I don't know whether the two of them slept that night, but somehow the cat came and ate while they weren't looking. Yoko was still camped out by the window the next morning, when Akira brought his camera over and started taking pictures of her.

"If she stops liking me, I might never see her again," he said. "I want to preserve as many images of her while it lasts."

I understood the way he felt, but it didn't strike me as a healthy way of looking at things. I would have told him to stop if I'd thought it would do any good. I remembered a story I'd heard once from Nagasaki, the filmmaker, about a time when he and Akira had said goodbye at Shinjuku station and made their separate ways to different trains. From his platform, Nagasaki had caught sight of Akira walking, alone and lost, and according to Nagasaki, looking as though he had suddenly aged at least ten years. I didn't want to peer too deeply into Akira's soul—that would be no fun for either of us—so I decided not to think too much about it. Instead I wondered what effects he would achieve with these new pictures of Yoko—this, after all, was a man who had managed to imbue his self-portrait photos with a presence that was almost overwhelming.

Yoko went home later that day to fetch a change of clothes, but soon came back again. Akira, of course, never went anywhere without his bag of clothes, and now that he'd found Yoko was apparently quite happy for the two of them to move in with me. And so it happened that I now had two new roommates.

We kept up the same sleeping arrangements. I slept alone in one room while Akira and Yoko shared the other. They may have been sharing a room, but whether they were actually sleeping together I'm not sure. Yoko was still keeping watch by the window until the cat showed up; from the second night, I had a distinct impression that Akira was no longer eager to help. But he was kept dangling. Somehow the cat managed to evade Yoko again on the second night, and then again on the third, until finally at some point during the fourth night, Yoko burst into the room where I was fast asleep and cried out in joy: "He came! The cat just came and ate!

"He's black, with white bits on his face and paws. He's one of those, what do you call them—panda cats. But this one's more like a pig the way he eats."

So it wasn't an orange-and-white tabby after all?

"He must have been gorging himself at all the houses in the neighborhood to get so fat like that. But they're really cute when they're eating, especially when you're looking down on them. All curled up in a ball, and so polite and well-behaved, with their little heads moving back and forth. He was totally into it." She took a breath, and then spoke up again. "What was that you said just now? About the orange-and-white one?"

I was surprised she hadn't picked up on it right away. Maybe she was too caught up in her own excitement to hear what I had said; or maybe she was simply more absent-minded than I had realized—she had gone three whole nights without managing a single sighting of the cat, after all. Or perhaps I was still half-asleep, and was merely imagining that I had mentioned the orange-and-white cat. Maybe the words hadn't actually crossed my lips at all. I was almost relieved to hear her ask about my comment, and I went on to fill her in on the story so far.

"Starting tomorrow," she said after I had finished, "I am going to look for that cat until I find him." She sounded pretty happy to have something to do with her days, but poor Akira, who had appeared by our side while I was telling the story, had nothing to contribute to the topic. He stood by Yoko's side in silence. Sure enough, starting from the following day, Yoko made it her habit to walk around the neighborhood with a tin of cat food and a packet of dried sardines, while Akira traipsed solemnly behind her with his camera.

What were my two new roommates doing to support themselves? Nothing; the money for their food came out of my salary. Neither of them cost much to support. Yoko spent her time either waiting by the window for cats, or trawling the neighborhood in search of the orange-and-white kitten. Akira did nothing but follow Yoko around taking pictures of her wherever she went. My salary was more than enough.

In fact, since Yoko did all the shopping and cooking, I was probably saving money, since I wasn't eating out the way I usually did. Akira seemed to get all the film he could use for free, and got his prints developed at a place run by a friend, so that didn't cost him anything either. And luckily enough, I had just been given a raise in April. It occurred to me that the whole point of having money was to allow people to live free and comfortable lives like the ones we were living now. I started to appreciate it for the first time in my life.

I was still going to the races with Ishigami every weekend. The big Derby race was coming up at the end of May, and the NHK Cup was held at the beginning of the month as a sort of warm-up for the big event.

By October every year the racecourse grass starts to turn from green to yellow and eventually loses its color entirely until it looks like flattened earth, before gaining a fresh growth of green when spring arrives, just in time for the NHK Cup in early May. But I didn't go to the races to admire the turf, nor did I usually pay much attention to the shifting color of the grass throughout the season, so that it came as quite a surprise when I turned up one day to find the whole course dyed a deep, rich green. It was the Sunday of the NHK Cup. There had been rain the night before, and the course shone a fresh and invigorating green.

We were more or less breaking even with our betting when the main race of the day came around. I liked the look of a horse from Kansai called Rugby Ball that was appearing in Tokyo for the first time, and hinted to Ishigami that I was thinking of putting quite a big stake on him.

"What kind of name is that for a horse—Rugby Ball? They're not even trying. Anything would be better than that."

This was one of Ishigami's little obsessions. It upset him to see Japanese racing moving away from European traditions. His attitude was exactly the opposite of Mitani's. Mitani didn't look for truth or realism in horse racing, and never thought of the horses' names at all except as material for his conspiracy theories.

"What's wrong with names like Divine Gift, or Never Say Die? Rugby Ball? They're just not thinking," he continued. And there was no doubt that a lot of the foreign-raised horses did have some impressive names. Never Say Die was a good one, as was the name of its foal, Die Hard. But personally, I didn't think Rugby Ball was as bad as Ishigami was making it out to be.

"Rugby Ball's owner is Odagiri Yuichi—the same owner who put out that horse Noah's Ark last year. He's the son of a literary critic, Odagiri something or other—Hideo or Susumu or something like that."

My racing knowledge now spread far beyond the confines of the course.

"He should be able to come up with a better name than that, then."

"Something out of one of the old poetry anthologies, you mean. From the Man'yoshu or something?"

"God, no. Nothing like that . . ."

We carried on our bumbling conversation as we wandered the course. It felt like rain again, and I remembered what I'd seen on the news about an accident in the nuclear power station at Chernobyl in the Soviet Union. I mentioned it to Ishigami. "Apparently we don't need to worry about the rain for another week or so here," he said, surprising me by giving a serious and considered reply for once.

I had expected him to give another of his usual remarks. "It's all over for us now," or something like that. Probably the only reason he didn't react this way was because I'd spoken of the weather as if it were nothing to worry about. Now my thoughts turned to the possibility that radiation sickness might affect the horses; since the accident had happened in the Soviet Union, the risk would be biggest in the North—and Hokkaido and Aomori were the traditional centers of horse breeding in Japan. Wasn't there a chance that the next generation of horses would grow up eating the polluted grass of those northern pastures and end up weak and emaciated as a result?

"You never know. There might be some kind of genetic mutation that makes them super-strong or something," Ishigami replied, half of him not caring either way, the other half apparently seriously considering the possibility that genetic mutations might make the horses stronger in the future.

This answer, or this way of thinking about things, was typical of Ishigami; even now, I sometimes think back on those days and wonder what it was that gave his casual remarks their unique brand of optimism and brightness. Whenever he sounded this note in our conversation, it brought to a halt whatever train of thought had been passing through my head and sent it flying off into space.

A few days later I was out drinking till late—a rarity in those days—and when I got home I found Akira listening to records in my room. I got the feeling he'd been waiting up for me. Probably he had only put the record on when he heard me coming, to make it look as though he was just taking it easy and hadn't been anxious for me to come back at all. There was an obsequious look in his eyes that wasn't normally there.

"You're home late tonight. I kept the evening free, thinking we'd finally get to catch up properly," he said, using the strange, patronizing tone of voice he tended to put on when he was feeling lonely or neglected. I ignored him and changed my clothes, then went to the bathroom to wash up. Akira stood behind me, a close-lipped smile on his face as he pecked and pinched at my back and nagged at me for attention.

"What's up with you—not getting enough or something?" I said. Akira laughed out loud. "Why are you always so mean?" he said, contorting his face into one of the most exaggerated displays of hurt I'd ever seen. But the servility had vanished from his eyes; he was back to his usual self now.

"You not getting any?" I asked again.

"She won't let me do any of that."

"Never mind what she lets you do. Are you having sex or not?"

"Uh, no, I guess not."

"In all this time?"

"What do you mean?"

"Have you not done it even once in all this time?"

"We did it twice."

"Well, there you go then. Good for you."

"Uh, three times actually."

"See, that's good."

"But that's what I'm trying to tell you. It's not good at all."

"Some guys spend ten thousand yen on a massage and get nothing but a hand job, so count yourself lucky."

"I don't have that kind of money."

"But for you it was free, right?"

"Of course. The girls love me."

"Well, there you go. Even better."

"But that's what I mean. It's not good at all."

"Try to think about something else then."

Maybe he was having problems getting it up? I managed to stop myself before the words came out.

The two of us were silent for a moment. Akira scratched his head childishly and said, "I'm going to take some pictures, I'll be right back." He headed toward the room where Yoko was sleeping.

I stayed up for a while wasting time with Akira, and by the time I went to bed it was already getting light. I woke up to the sound of Yoko coming back from looking for the kitten.

"I can't find him anywhere," she said. I raised my head from the futon when I heard her coming through the door, and was impressed to see Akira standing behind her with his camera as usual. So impressed, in fact, that I made a sudden proposal.

"Hey, why don't we head over to the Toshimaen amusement park today?"

Akira practically jumped over Yoko in his excitement. He rushed over to where I was lying and tore the covers away. "Let's go, let's go. Come on, let's go now!"

But I still wasn't properly awake, and I struggled for another half an hour or so with the blankets, and Akira, and sleepiness, washing my face with movements so sluggish they frustrated even me, before sitting down and taking my time sipping the coffee Yoko had made. Only then did I feel sufficiently awake to consider leaving the house. By the time I was ready it was past noon.

"Sorry I took so long," I said to Akira, but he was so excited by the thought of where we were going and the novelty of this unexpected excursion that he was completely unperturbed.

"Yeah, you're really slow," he said, picking up his camera and leading the way. In his hand was a plastic supermarket bag containing Yoko's packet of dried sardines, a can of cat food, and a can opener.

It was a beautiful spring day; the sky was blue and cloudless, with just a gentle breeze in the air to keep things from getting uncomfortably hot. It was close to perfect; I felt my cares slip away as the pores in my skin opened up to welcome the spring. Just being outside on a day like this was a treat—the thought that we were heading for an amusement park was enough to make me itchy with anticipation.

As we walked I asked Akira whether he ever asked Yoko to pose for the pictures he was always taking of her.

"No. I just take them," he said. It was pretty much the answer I'd been expecting.

"I'd like to see them some time," I said.

"No way. I'm not showing them to anyone." This was typical of Akira: he would grow attached to anyone who was brusque with him, and start putting on airs whenever you tried to get close.

"Besides, I'm going to make a special exhibit of them soon. Imagine that—nothing but these huge pictures of Yoko covering the whole room."

After a while we came to the apartment building where I'd last seen the kitten. The cherry tree that had been in full bloom was now covered in green leaves. I was standing and looking up into the tree when Yoko jogged over to the base of the trunk. This was where she'd left her can of cat food. She checked inside the can and then made her announcement. "He's not eaten anything yet today!"

"Well, you only just left it there."

"But it's been nearly two hours now."

"And normally it gets eaten?"

"Yeah. But it could be that fat panda cat again for all I know. I don't mind, though, even if it is the fat panda—better than nothing. Sometimes, though, the whole thing's gone—the can and everything. I bet the building caretaker hates cats."

It was from Yoko that I learned for the first time how few apartments in Tokyo allow residents to keep cats as pets. It had never occurred to me that anyone would bother to put a clause in a lease specifying that no cats or dogs were allowed on the premises.

"Everyone keeps them in secret," Yoko said. It figured. I hadn't known this fact before, though my life was not going to change much now that I did.

"Are we planning to walk the whole way there or something?" Akira wailed suddenly. There was no room in his mind for any other subject. That was fine by me; at least it meant we'd have something to talk about other than cats.

"It's only an hour or so."

"Wow, we're really walking that far?"

"I am. I like walking. And you walked all the way from Ikebukuro that time. In February."

"Yeah, but Yoko . . ."

Akira didn't get to finish his sentence. Just then we came across a small shop with a banner fluttering outside advertising the rice cakes and sweets traditionally eaten for Children's Day at the start of May.

"Hey, let's get some for the journey," he said.

I couldn't remember the last time I'd been in a confectionery store, but I had a fairly good idea of what to expect; Akira, on the other hand, seemed to be encountering the concept for the first time.

He reacted to the place in wonder, as if he'd never seen such strange and wondrous things in his life, occasionally making childlike comments on the funny things he found. "Look at this one, it's all lumpy. Creepy." Yoko added her own explanations, telling us the name of each one.

"Those are called fawns," she said.

Akira pointed out what he wanted, and we ended up buying three each of five different kinds of sweet rice cakes: *kashiwa-mochi, ka-no-ko, domyoji, kusa-dango,* and some round balls covered in a kind of thick, sweet, and salty sauce. Yoko noticed as Akira pointed to what he wanted that his fingernails were long and caked in dirt, and made him go into a *pachinko* parlor in front of the shop to wash his hands. She stood next to him and supervised. "Will we really be able to eat all these?" she asked.

But we weren't even back on the main street before Akira ripped the bag open and stuffed one of the *kashiwa-mochi* into his mouth. He munched on it manically, and gulped it down whole. I ate one too, and then we helped ourselves to a *ka-no-ko* and a *domyoji* each. The question wasn't whether we'd be able to eat all we'd bought: had we bought enough?

I expected Yoko to make some comments about our gluttony, but now that I'd finished eating I realized that Yoko wasn't the kind to get scandalized or amused by such behavior. If she had been, there was no way she would have been able to spend whole days at a time with Akira—that much was for sure.

We agreed to save the rest for once we got to the park, and continued walking. After a while, Yoko spotted a white cat sitting on top of a fence by the side of the road.

"Look at that kitty—white all over," she said. She stopped to talk to the cat. "Soaking up some rays, kitty? I bet that feels good."

"Look, he's such a fluffster," she said, turning round to us with a smile.

This seemed to be a term that Yoko had come up with herself to refer to happy, contented, daydreaming cats. Even hearing it for the first time, it was clear enough what she meant by the term when one of these "fluffsters" was right there in front of you. The cat seemed to be in a friendly mood. He rolled over onto his back and started purring. Yoko took out some bonito flakes and held them in front of the cat's nose. He licked at them with relish.

"You're not a stray. You belong to somebody, don't you, kitty?" she said. Akira seemed less interested. "Come on, if we don't get going it will be closed by the time we get there," he said.

"Bye bye, kitty. Take care now," Yoko said, waving a quick good-bye to the cat on the wall.

Our route took us along back streets and alleyways—classic cat territory. Yoko stopped to say hello to every cat we came across, but only one of them was friendly. From Akira's point of view, it was probably a blessing that the other cats we encountered were too suspicious to want to make friends. Even the one friendly cat we saw must have drawn out the time painfully for him.

The friendly cat was sitting and licking himself on a patch of grass by a wooden fence. He was a thin, dirty-looking specimen, with black and brown blotches on his coat. This would have been enough to put me off the idea of making friends, but Yoko didn't discriminate. She crouched down and held a finger to its nose. Once they'd made friends, she started to feed the cat bonito flakes. Akira stood to one side looking bored. He took the last *kashiwa-mochi* from the bag and shoved most of it into his mouth. Then he took what little was left of it and held it out in front of the cat.

"Here, this is for you," he said.

But the cat ignored him, and carried on eating the bonito flakes from Yoko's hand.

"You don't want to eat that, do you, kitty?" she said. Akira shrugged his shoulders and shoved the rest of the *mochi* into his mouth, even though he was still working on his previous mouthful.

After an hour or so, we finally caught sight of the Shuttle Loop roller coaster inside the Toshimaen amusement park.

"Look, there it is. That's it, right? Toshimaen? Come on, let's climb in over the wall," Akira said. But even his high spirits couldn't obscure the fact that there was barbed wire on top of the walls—and it would have felt weird climbing over the walls in broad daylight anyway, so we decided to keep walking around the perimeter until we came to the official entrance, or at least to a point where we might be able to scale the wall more comfortably.

There was a row of houses on the other side of the road. It had never occurred to me before to wonder what it would be like to live so close to an amusement park. It was easy enough to imagine the advantages of living near the beach, but with an amusement park it was hard to see how the pluses would outweigh the minuses. My reverie was interrupted by Yoko.

"They have a big fireworks display here every week during the summer, don't they? That means if you live in one of these houses you get to see fireworks every week. How weird."

"Let's come again in the summer," Akira said. "It's too bad you didn't rent an apartment round here; it would have been way more fun than being out in the middle of nowhere where you are now," he added, nattering away but still keeping his mind more or less on the task at hand, which was to find a spot without barbed wire where Yoko might be able to scale the wall.

Judging by how far we still were from the tower on the Shuttle Loop roller coaster we had seen, it was clear that we'd arrived at the point farthest away from where the actual rides and amusements were. Even after we'd walked along the wall for another 15 minutes, the big tower was still the only thing we could see. Gradually, more things came into view, and for the first time I started to feel for the first time that we really were drawing close to an amusement park.

Even so, there were no shouts and screams—maybe that was just the way things were on a weekday; but it was enough to give me the inkling of a bad feeling that I couldn't quite put into words until Akira spoke up and said: "It's so quiet." And then, "Are you sure this place is open every day?"

The idea hadn't even occurred to me till Akira asked the question.

"I think so," I said. My lips moved of their own accord, apparently much more confident about this than I was. It occurred to me that not once had we seen a roller coaster full of screaming people go either up or down that big tower we'd been looking at for so long, and I was now more desperate than ever to get inside and find out for sure. We finally came to an isolated spot where there were no passers-by and climbed in over the wall—Akira first, then Yoko, and then me.

We came down next to a fenced-off pool area, with the roller coaster rails running above our heads. There was no one in the pool—not surprising, given that it was still only the middle of

May—but there was no ignoring the sense of foreboding we all felt at the complete lack of any sound whatsoever from the roller-coaster rails overhead. As we walked further into the park it became clear beyond any shadow of doubt that the park was closed.

"Too bad," I told Akira, in a tone that was half apology and half consolation. He was obviously disappointed, but remained surprisingly upbeat in spite of everything.

"So this is what an amusement park looks like, huh? It's my first time. Next time, let's come when everything's working," he said, looking around excitedly, taking everything in. Maybe because he was seeing things for the first time and didn't know what they were like when they were actually running, Akira didn't ask the kind of insistent questions he normally asked, gazing instead at the Flying Pirates ride and the Corkscrew in silent longing and awe, opening his mouth only to voice delight at what he saw. "Wow" was about the extent of it.

We finished our tour of the park and sat down on a bench near the Shuttle Loop to eat the last of the sweets. Akira wolfed down most of Yoko's share as well. A cool May evening breeze began to blow. Yoko looked up at the sky. "Ah, that feels nice," she said. She certainly sounded at one with the world. I don't know what possessed me to ask such a dumb question, but I found myself asking Yoko, "Have you ever been really unhappy?"

"You mean like when something really bad happened to me? I don't think so," she said. She made it sound obvious.

"What about a really bad person?" I asked.

"I don't remember anyone in particular," she said. She sounded so carefree that I had to take her answers at face value. I heard the shutter of Akira's camera, but Yoko showed no reaction. She must have been used to the sound by now.

We meandered our way out of the park, eventually emerging by the front entrance. Not once did we meet a security guard or anyone cleaning up. Nothing bad happened at all—maybe Yoko's good luck was rubbing off on us, or maybe it was Akira's. Akira, in fact, seemed to be an almost supernaturally lucky person. He had never been caught breaking the rules, although he had shop-lifted, fled from restaurants without paying, and run away from plenty of taxi drivers in his time. Just being around him made me feel lucky.

The Toshimaen station on the Seibu line was right in front of the main entrance. Akira and Yoko took the outward-bound train and changed at Nerima, the first station, for the train back home to my apartment; I decided to head in the opposite direction, toward the city and work.

I woke up the next morning to find Yoko already preparing break-fast in the kitchen. This was part of our daily routine by now.

Akira emerged soon after and made his way to the kitchen. He paused on his way and gave me a huge grin and the thumbs-up. I assumed he'd finally persuaded Yoko to sleep with him again. Good for him. Here I was, feeding these two people out of my salary and now apparently looking after their love life too. The reality that I had entered my thirties hit me like a hammer. Maybe I should have felt aggrieved at the way things were happening—there didn't seem to be much in it for me, after all—but surpris-ingly (or not) I had no interest in Akira's sex life, and couldn't really get too worked up about whether having them live with me was in my best interests or not either. Maybe it was the weather that was making me feel this way. It was another bright sunny May morning—splinters of light seemed to fill the room—and a gentle breeze blew through the open window. But no—I knew it was something more than that. The way I related to my surroundings had changed.

Yoko picked up her bonito flakes and a can of cat food and left the house with me for the first of her searches for the orange-and-white kitten, Akira lagging behind with his camera. This was nothing out of the ordinary for them; Yoko left the house around nine every morning. What I hadn't known until now was that this was only the first of at least three, and sometimes as many as six or seven, daily outings to look for the cat. We walked together for a while. "Thanks to my exploring, I know all the back alleys around here pretty well by now," Yoko said.

"And you still haven't seen the orange-and-white cat?" I said.

"I know." It was a verbal shrug of the shoulders, nothing more. The whole thing reminded me of a story I'd heard once about a relative of mine whose dog carried its bowl out of the house every day and left it somewhere in the garden. When feeding time came, the dog's owner strode out into the garden saying, "All right, so where have you hidden your bowl today?" and the dog followed behind, sniffing at his backside. It occurred to me that the dog's barked replies would not have been unlike those that Yoko was giving me now, and the thought brought a smile to my face.

"But I always meet lots of other cats," Yoko said. "There're loads of cats around here. I've made friends with about ten already, and you know there could always be another one waiting around the corner at any moment," she burbled.

Before long we came to the apartment building where I'd last seen the kitten. The cherry tree was even greener and more beautiful now than it had been yesterday, glinting in the bright morning sunshine. Every glistening leaf on the tree reflected the sunlight, the leaves rippling like little waves of light whenever the branches swayed in the breeze. The can under the tree was empty, its tin glinting cleanly in the sun.

"Wow," I said.

"Yeah, I changed it for a new one last night," Yoko said with a laugh. "I hope it really is the little orange-and-white one that's eating it," she added. I could tell by the way she said it that she was pretty sure.

My mind drifted back to the time I had watched the cherry blossoms dancing to the ground where the empty can sat now. I could almost see the orange-and-white cat sitting there eating the bonito flakes. He was already quite big the last time I saw him, but in my mind he was still the same size he had been that first time he came and peeped into my apartment through the sliding screen. How delighted Yoko would have been if she could have seen him then, I thought.

My own interest in cats was nothing compared to Yoko's. Even where "my" orange-and-white kitten was concerned, it was Yoko who spent her days looking for it, while I did nothing. Partly this was because I naturally tended to step back a bit whenever I saw someone as intently focused as Yoko was on looking for the kitten.

I don't think I've known anyone to do anything as devotedly and attentively as Yoko, or with so little pretentiousness or affectation. Usually, people do their best to hide how passionate they are about something, or feel embarrassed about it. It's a kind of canniness you often come across in people who are trying hard. There's something mean and depressing about it, like watching a person with no talent trying to outwit someone better than himself. With Yoko there was none of this. She was fresh and naïve and pure, and being with her made me grow impatient with some of the more calculating and diffident aspects of my own character. As I watched how she went about things, and saw more of the infectious enthusiasm that she brought to bear on every aspect of her life, I became aware of the weaknesses and faults in my own approach to life. But at this stage I still tended to keep slightly detached from her unrestrained enthusiasm.

But there was another reason. Late May was the apex of the horse racing season: the Derby. I was obsessed with racing in those days, and for fans of the turf, the Derby has a significance all of its own. No other race comes close.

Race horses normally run their first races in the fall of their third year, and reach their peak for the Derby in the year they turn four. In a sense, all the other races a horse runs are nothing more than preparation for the Derby in its fourth year. Around ten thousand thoroughbreds with the potential to become racehorses are born in Japan alone each year. Their training starts when they are three years old, and many of them drop out early. The horses that do make it through training compete against each other in a series of races of ascending levels—starting with the Newcomers'

Race for horses running competitively for the first time, and culminating with the Derby itself, the absolute pinnacle of the horse racing pyramid.

I read somewhere once that the Derby will normally mark the ten-thousandth race in the calendar year, including JRA races and local events. There's a certain poetic drama to the idea: ten thousand thoroughbreds, ten thousand races, one Derby. But of course no one could ever really know how many races are run every year up and down the country. Probably it's just the horse racing equivalent of an urban legend—but I've always liked the story, even if it has no basis in fact. The story comes back to me every year when the time for the Derby draws near, putting an extra spring in my step and getting my heart to beat just a little bit faster.

Nothing in baseball comes close to the importance the Derby has in horse racing. When it comes down to it, the game that determines a pro baseball championship is just one of 130 or so games played over the course of a long season, and the matchups that mark the high school championships held at Koshien Stadium every summer are just games that finish when one team or the other wins. The Derby is something completely different.

Of course the Derby is a system just like any other—there never has been and never will be a year in which "No Suitable Derby Winner" is declared. The race must be won by one of the horses competing, and in this sense the Derby may seem to resemble a baseball competition in which one or other of the teams that have entered is bound to win. But that isn't the way it feels to the fans. For us, one of the things that make the Derby unique is the tendency of the race to produce what seems in retrospect to have been inevitable winners. This sounds ridiculous even to me now when I say it, but (allowing for a little exaggeration) the facts are just as I have described them. I always feel a special kind of excitement as Derby day approaches.

But the idea that a Derby winner is swept forward by fate (and the fact that another name has been added to the legendary roster of Derby winners) is not quite the same thing as saying that the best horse always wins the race, as someone like Ishigami—who lived his life at a safe distance from excitement of all kinds—well understood.

This was perhaps why Ishigami showed no interest in the idea that Rugby Ball was now a strong contender for the Derby, based on his impressive performance in the race we had attended together at the start of May, and that he would carry on winning right through to the big day itself. And this time around, Ishigami's dislike of the horse was nothing to do with his ridiculous name.

"It doesn't work like that. A horse doesn't win his first three races and then go straight on to take the Derby in his fourth. So we know now that Rugby Ball is a good runner, fine—but that's not the kind of horse that wins the Derby. With a Derby winner, it's only after the race that you think: Yeah, I should have known he would win, that's a pretty good horse." This was typical of the way Ishigami looked at things.

If Rugby Ball won each of his first four races, and ended up becoming Derby winner as a result, he would become a national sensation. And that's what didn't seem right to Ishigami. There was such a thing as a person whose talents were too obvious. It wasn't always the person with the special gifts who rose to the top;

sometimes a person with weaknesses in certain areas was more likely to succeed. It was almost as though what you really needed to make it to the top was not so much talent itself as . . . as this thing, whatever it was, that saved you from standing out too much from the crowd. At least, that's the way he saw it.

"You don't notice the horse at all until he wins. Often it doesn't seem to be going well at all at first—but when he gets to the finish line, there he is: a head or half a length ahead of everyone else." Ishigami couldn't help looking a little foolish as he stretched his neck out as he talked, like a horse reaching for the finish line. "You can't even say for sure what it is that makes the horse a good one. That's the kind you want."

A look of satisfaction came over his face as he closed his case.

Certain ways of winning a race made a horse stand out, and others didn't. Anyone could see how strong a horse like Rugby Ball was when he surged away from the pack and galloped home alone. A horse that won after a last-minute dash from the back of the pack as the finish line approached was even more likely to impress. There were also those rare but heart-warming occasions when a horse would lead the field from the start line to the finish line, galloping away from the pack and never once losing the lead till it crossed the finish line. But the horse Ishigami had his eye on, Dynamo Gulliver, never won in any of these ways. He would lumber unimpressively from one end of the course to the other, never attracting any special attention or praise—in fact, the only thing you could remember about him when it was all over was that he had won the race.

Dynamo Gulliver only ever won by unexceptional distances: half a length or so. When a horse streaked out ahead of the others and won by a distance, this was clear proof that it was the strongest runner in the field. Conversely, a horse that beat the runner-up by just a nose's length, so that you had to peer endlessly at a photo finish before you could confirm that he had indeed finished first—this too was proof of that all-important winning instinct. With Dynamo Gulliver, it was half a length or nothing.

But nobody disputed the fact that Dynamo Gulliver was a good horse, and nobody would be surprised if he really did win the Derby. In fact, if he did, then everybody would be sure to think it was no surprise—"That was a good horse," they would say, and he would justly join the illustrious ranks of Derby winners. That's what Ishigami had meant, and I knew that he hadn't intended to single this horse out for special praise or criticism—he was just talking of Dynamo Gulliver as a typical case of how a horse came to stand at the pinnacle of the racing system.

The words he had spoken were simple enough, and he probably wasn't thinking about things too deeply himself at the time. I certainly didn't assign any particularly profound interpretation to his comments when I heard them. But for various reasons what he said made quite an impression on me, and I had a feeling that I would have cause to remember his words many times in the days and weeks to come.

Four days later it was Derby day, and Ishigami and I watched together as Dynamo Gulliver lumbered along with the rest of the pack for the first half of the race, only to pull ahead at the end, eventually coming in the winner by—half a length. The sight of him galloping across the finish line ahead of all the other horses on the biggest stage of them all made me shout out his name in excitement.

That's how it is with the races: The reasoning you've put hours of time into (many dozens of hours, sometimes) is tested and weighed in the balance when the race is run. There's no room for weaseling your way out of it by contending that the outcome might have been different if they ran the race again. It makes no sense to imagine a different result. As it happened on this occasion, the winner was precisely the kind of horse that Ishigami had predicted. Because of this, his words have stuck with me, and I have often remembered them and replayed them to myself in one form or another in the years that have passed since.

3

Not long after the Derby—not that the Derby had anything to do with Akira or Yoko, or with any aspect of our daily life at the time, really, beyond providing proof (as if any were needed) of the extent to which my memories of those days are marked and measured out in terms of horse racing events—anyway, it was not long after Dynamo Gulliver won the Derby that Akira started to go out alone to hang out with his fellow filmmakers whenever they got together in Shinjuku or other places around town. I interpreted this to mean that, as far as he was concerned, his relationship with Yoko was going all right.

Despite this change in Akira's life, Yoko's daily routine continued as before. She was still putting out cat food offerings in front of the apartment every day before making her several daily excursions in search of the orange-and-white kitten. I did once suggest that she should stop going out at night now that Akira was no longer around to accompany her, but she didn't seem concerned about her safety at all.

"It's cool. I only go as far as that building and back," she said, though I knew for a fact she was making new detours every time she went out.

Akira was out and Yoko was alone in front of the apartment the night we finally found the orange-and-white cat. I was walking past the building when Yoko hurried over on tiptoe to tell me what had happened.

The orange-and-white cat was where Yoko always left the food. He was a lot bigger now than when I had last seen him, and didn't look much like a kitten at all anymore. I suppose this shouldn't have come as any surprise. I'd first spotted him back in February, which would make him—I did the calculation quickly in my head—at least six months old by now.

But the former kitten was still sleek and smart, with none of the roly-poly puffiness of a fat cat. This came as a relief, since I had been more or less obsessed with the animal since its kittenhood. Of course I was probably biased in favor of this particular orange-and-white cat, but I've always found sleek and well-balanced cats much more attractive than fat ones, and there's no doubt in my mind that a cat who still retains signs of his days as a kitten is way cuter than one that has grown once and for all into an adult. And no cat ever looked cuter than my little orange-and-white kitten did now as he looked up at us cautiously and lapped at his food.

"Wow, he's a real cutie," Yoko said. "I wish I could have seen him when he was still a kitten. You were so lucky to see him then." She turned back to the cat.

"You're really hungry, aren't you kitty? You go ahead and help yourself. Eat as much as you want till you're nice and full." Her voice when she spoke to cats was nothing like her usual flat, who-gives-a-shit monotone. It positively dripped with feeling. I remembered noticing the same thing on our way to the amusement park, but the change hadn't been as dramatic then, perhaps because Akira had been with us too.

"Such a good little boy, aren't you, kitty? Look at you, sitting there all prim and proper. I hope the other strays don't pick on you for being too well-brought-up."

She broke off for a moment and turned to face me.

"I'm so glad we finally found him. It's been so long I thought we'd never find him. I started to wonder, what if he's dead or something?" She turned back to the cat. "But here you are, alive and well."

The cat's tongue darted out and snatched some more food into his mouth. Yoko was watching intently, apparently determined not to miss a thing.

"Look at the way he eats. Look at his paws. They're *so* sweet. Like two little hands."

The cat suddenly stopped eating. He shrunk back and turned around. We both assumed he was about to disappear again, when Yoko suddenly pointed toward a bush behind the cat. "Look, there's another one," she said. And then I saw it too—another diminutive orange-and-white cat. His pattern was almost exactly the same as the one we'd been looking for all this time. I bet they're related, I thought as I watched the first cat walk slowly over to the bush where the other cat was hiding. The second cat came out from the bush as if drawn out by the example of the first, and came over to stand by the cat food. The two of them circled the food warily as we watched, an atmosphere of intimacy and familiarity evident between them. Apart from an occasional sigh, we stood in silence and watched.

Both cats had tails almost as long as the rest of their bodies. The first cat flicked his grandly from side to side as he walked, his tail stretched straight along the length of his back, while the new arrival, still more cautious and still on his guard, kept his low to the ground. After a while, the second cat lowered his head to the food and took a few mouthfuls, while the first cat prowled around cautiously as if keeping guard.

But the second cat didn't eat for long. After a few bites at the food he stepped away from the can and fell in line with the first cat, as if drawing close to him for protection. It was only now that we realized that the first cat was a good deal bigger than his brother.

"The second one's too shy and scared," Yoko said, still looking straight ahead at the cats. "He's too frightened to come and eat—that's why he's so tiny." She decided to take things into her own hands by talking to the cats directly. "It's all right, little one. We're not going to hurt you. Just relax and eat as much as you want."

After a while the first cat put his head back to the can of food and started eating again. The second cat stuck close to the first, occasionally bending down to catch a bite of food when the first cat raised his head, his eyes darting up at us and his surroundings all the time as he ate. The second cat lifted his head from the can and we noticed that the can was empty. Yoko pulled a new, unopened can from her bag, along with a can opener, which she used to open the new can.

"Luckily I always carry two cans with me, just in case."

"That's what I call being prepared."

"It's nothing to do with being prepared. It's called having a heart. If you really love someone, you have to show it. It's not the thought that counts, you know," Yoko said happily as she scooped half the contents into the empty can with a spoon she had brought along with everything else, and set the second course down gently on the ground in front of the cats.

The two cats were standing a step or two back from the empty can and looking up at us warily. They reacted to Yoko's movements by pinning their ears back and watching us suspiciously, but the first cat stepped forward and put his face to the can almost as soon as Yoko set it down on the ground, before turning around to the other cat, who stepped forward at this sign of encouragement and began to eat. He seemed a little more relaxed now.

"That's so cool, the way he takes care of the other one like that," Yoko said. I nodded, and realized that the smaller cat had probably not been far away the first time I fed the bonito flakes to his big brother, presumably looking on from a hiding place in the bushes.

I think it was probably because Yoko was with me this time that I decided we had better give the cats names to help us differentiate between them. It wasn't so much a question of what was convenient for us; it just felt like the right thing to do.

"How about we call them Kitty and Catty," I suggested.

"That's not cute enough. Let's call them little Mew and little Miao," Yoko answered right away—she must have been thinking the same thing all along. Her suggestion was fine by me, and we stood for a while longer watching Mew and Miao as they continued their meal. When they had all but finished the second can, they slinked off and disappeared into the bushes. We watched them go.

"That's the thing about cats," I said. "They eat your food and then just take off without even saying thanks."

"The fact that they eat your food is their way of saying thanks."

"That was some thank you they gave us then."

"Right. It's cats' thank-yous that make the world go round."

"And to think I never even knew."

Chatting lightheartedly about what we'd just seen, we made our way back to the apartment.

It seemed to be a rule that every time I saw Mew and Miao, someone else would move into my apartment. The day after Yoko and I saw the two cats, who should turn up at my apartment again but Shimada.

This time things were more serious than when he had come to stay in the early spring. Apparently he had suddenly received news that the building where he was living was about to be demolished. He didn't have much in the way of possessions, but even Shimada owned a few things. He'd sent half of his belongings down to his parents' place in Kyushu, then thrown away almost everything else. He arrived at my apartment with two suitcases and a paper bag.

According to Shimada, the news had come out of the blue. "The landlord just told me I was going to have to leave four days ago. Says they're pulling the building down week after next, so I've got to get out." Shimada's building was a tatty and worn-down hovel of decrepit rubble, where the tatami mats on the floor were not just worn through but actually warped from the damp. Even so, it was hard to believe that anyone would knock down a building with just a few days' notice.

Four or five of Shimada's friends had made this their fortress two years ago—including Yada, the friend on whom he had thrown himself when he'd first moved to Tokyo—but the only ones left there now were Shimada and a man in his fifties. What he did with his life I have no idea. The likeliest explanation was that the landlord had warned Shimada of what was going to happen several times, but Shimada simply hadn't understood what he said. Not that it made much difference at this stage. Had he at least made sure that he was paid compensation?

"Well, he gave me my deposit back. He mumbled something or other about the other stuff, but that guy goes on and on sometimes. You can't follow a word he says."

I found it hard to believe that anyone would have the gall to ask for a deposit on a dump that like, but Shimada seemed to think nothing of it.

"He's selling it off for redevelopment. Some people get a million yen for being evicted in cases like that, you know."

Shimada blanched.

"Are you serious?" It was not Shimada himself who shouted this last question, but Akira.

Once Shimada established that he'd be earning a certain level of income, he showed no interest in earning any more. The change I'd noticed in his eyes when I mentioned the figure of a million yen was like a reflex that still survived from the days when he had no money, and went against the way he really felt about financial questions now. At least that's how I interpreted it—probably because I felt the same way on the subject myself; now that I was supporting Akira and Yoko on my salary, I had just about the right amount, but if they had suddenly announced they were moving on and I found myself on my own again, it wouldn't have bothered me at all if my salary had suddenly been cut.

And so it happened that Shimada came to live in my apartment for a while. He took to sleeping on the floor next to my bed. The only difference in his behavior this time around was that weather was warmer now than when he'd come to stay before, so that he took his trousers off that first night and slept in his shirt and tie by my side. The following evening, Yoko came to me with a serious look on her face. Apparently the way the four of us were sharing the space wasn't right.

Here is what she had to say, more or less: The fact that she and Akira had been sharing a room up till now was not because they were boyfriend and girlfriend but because I had a right to a room of my own, where I could sleep undisturbed by the comings and goings of the various people who might come to stay. I was the owner of the apartment, after all. It wasn't right for me to have to share my room with Shimada simply because he had turned up as well—that meant I would lose my private space, something that was to be avoided at all costs. But then, it didn't seem quite right for her to share a room with Akira and Shimada either—and so she had decided that she would take her futon and sleep in the kitchen, leaving Akira and Shimada to share the spare room next to mine. This was apparently the best way to ensure that I continued to enjoy restful nights of uninterrupted solitude.

"But you can't just sleep on the bare floor. It's not good for you."

"I'll be fine. Besides, it's summer."

"But someone could come in through the door. And the kitchen's the first room they'd come to."

"That's not true. You can get straight into this room we're in now from the outside too. Besides, I've got three men here to look after me."

"You wouldn't be able to keep an eye out for the cat from the kitchen."

"That's okay. I can stay here by the window and watch until I get tired."

Yoko was obviously not going to back down. The only alternative I could come up with was to move my bed so that Yoko would at least have something other than bare floorboards to sleep on. Yoko was happy enough to go along with this, but the idea didn't seem to please Akira, who kept interrupting the whole time Yoko and I were discussing the details. "Why? Why does that have to happen? Why can't things just stay the way they are?" Shimada stood next to him, trying to calm him down. "It's all right," he said, "I'll find a place of my own soon. It's just for a week or two," he said to no one in particular. But Akira knew as well as anyone that Shimada had done nothing to look for a place of his own, and even he must have realized that Shimada was adept at adapting to a situation and taking in his stride whatever challenges life happened to throw his way.

Regardless of what Akira thought, though, things seemed to have been resolved, and Yoko started to get ready to go out with the cat food. This wasn't an expedition that required extensive preparations. All it really involved was putting an unopened tin of cat food in a plastic bag along with yesterday's leftovers and a can-opener, and putting on a sweater to keep herself warm. It didn't take more than a couple of minutes. But for Akira the time seemed to creep by as he weighed the unenviable options available to him, and tried to decide whether to stay behind with me to plead his case, or to stand up and follow Yoko.

In the end, the desire to spend even a few extra minutes with the woman who was leaving him to sleep alone in the kitchen won out. But as I looked at the worried expression on his face, it occurred to me that his carefree days were about to end. To an outsider, there was something comical about the distress on his face.

"Where's she off to?" Shimada asked me once the two of them had left. I decided to keep things brief, and muttered a few words about "some cat."

As I'd expected, Shimada showed no more concern for the matter, beyond a grunt of uninterested surprise. He got up and moved his futon over and started to get ready for bed. I found myself saying, "I guess you don't feel like finding a place to live right away, do you?" His ambiguous smile was enough to confirm my suspicions. I wasn't sure myself whether I was asking the question in lieu of wishing him good night or if I was inviting him to have a whiskey or two with me before he went to sleep.

"It got so crowded there, with Yada-san and all the rest of them coming and going the whole time," he said. The building he'd been living in was full of vacant apartments, and these were used by the filmmaking crowd on a semi-regular basis as a hangout spot. For Yada and the others the dilapidated apartment had become nothing more than a place to meet. Shimada was the only one still living there on a permanent basis. The rest of them apparently felt no hesitation about coming over whenever they wanted and staying up all night. I couldn't help thinking that Shimada might have used one of these empty apartments himself when his own room had been taken over for filming and saved himself the effort of coming all the way over to my apartment, though I could see how all the noise involved in a filming project might have made him want to get out of the way while it was going on. Also, his was the only room with any furniture in it—not that the furniture was much to write home about.

What had Shimada been doing till now whenever the crowd of filmmakers descended? Apparently, he would exchange brief hellos before retreating into his own room. Nothing so extraordinary about this, you might think: Except that Shimada himself had come all the way from Hokkaido to fulfill his ambition of becoming a Tokyo filmmaker.

"So it would just be the same thing all over again wherever I go," Shimada said. He obviously didn't mean it in a good sense.

"You'll just have to rent a bigger place," I said.

"I can't see the sense in spending forty or fifty thousand a month just on rent."

"I don't think you'd get much for that these days. I'm paying eighty-five for this place."

"You're kidding me."

"And that's relatively cheap. This is Nakamurabashi, you know. No express trains. Practically out in the sticks."

"Jeez."

His mind turned back to the apartment he'd just been evicted from. "They can't have been making much out of me at the last place, then. I was only paying thirteen thousand a month. I guess it makes sense that the landlord wanted to sell. More money in redevelopment than having me and that old guy in there."

He lived in a world of his own. Never mind selling the place off—thirteen thousand yen probably wouldn't even have covered the landlord's taxes. But I held my tongue. What difference did it make now anyway?

"Remember we used to play that game—All?"

I'd forgotten about it, but the memories came back to me now. We used to play it quite often back in the days when the old crowd shared the apartment. It was a gambling game—just about the simplest gambling game that could be played with a deck of cards. It would have been impossible for everyone to learn and remember the rules to a more complicated game like mah-jongg, and we knew that something like that would soon become boring and tedious anyway. "All" was anything but complex, and yet its simplicity gave it a unique kind of excitement. We would all start off betting small amounts. Five yen here, ten yen there. But it didn't take long for us to get carried away, and within five minutes the stakes were up to fifty thousand yen a game.

"I took a hundred thousand off Yamakawa one night."

"Yeah. He never came again after that."

"Funny. Did Akira used to play?"

"Only every day."

"But he never has any money."

"He did in those days. 'Cause he always won."

We reminisced about the old days until Akira and Yoko came back home.

A while later, once the four of us had filed off to our respective sleeping places—with Yoko staying put for the time being at the living room window waiting for the cat—I decided to call Yumiko to give her the report I'd been meaning to give her since Yoko and I had found the kittens two evenings earlier. I started off in my best diplomatic style by apologizing for calling late in the evening.

"I hope I didn't wake your baby by calling so late," I said.

"Don't worry about that. No child of mine is going to grow up high-strung like that, I hope. Anyway, what's this about that young man and his girlfriend you mentioned? I hear they're living under your roof and you're feeding them out of your own pocket?"

"I'm not feeding them; they're helping themselves to my food. There's a difference."

Our conversation soon turned to the cat. I mentioned how impressed I was that Yumiko had surmised two whole months ago that the little orange-and-white kitten I'd seen must have been one of a pair.

"It was only a hunch. I was just talking off the top of my head."

I believed her. But the fact that she had spoken without thinking didn't take away from the fact that she had, after all, been right—and it made me realize that I'd have found it much more difficult to get along with the kind of person who actually thought these things through and weighed her words carefully before giving her considered opinion. I certainly didn't expect seriousness of this kind from Yumiko.

"You mean to tell me that now *she's* the one going out looking for the kitten? Interesting girl."

"Yeah. Except it's not a kitten anymore. Actually, Yoko's sitting by the window right now, waiting for the cat to come and eat its food."

"Sounds like the kind of thing a cat would do," Yoko said. According to her, cats could stand stock still for long periods waiting for their prey in a way that would be unthinkable for most human beings.

"But for cats, that's their job."

"Maybe it's the same for her. Certainly sounds like she's taking it pretty seriously."

I tried to remember how Yumiko and I had passed the time when we were twenty—the age Yoko was now—but I couldn't remember a thing. Even if human beings were fated to forget by the time they turned thirty how they had spent their twentieth year on the planet, nevertheless, the fact was that twenty was a more significant time in a person's life than thirty. I started to wonder whether I ought to feel somehow responsible for the way Yoko was spending her days.

I wasn't going to say anything about it now, but I had the feeling that I would be talking this over with Yumiko sooner or later.

"Stray cats hardly ever get friendly with people. She'll just have to be satisfied with things the way they are." She meant that I should just leave the cat to do what it wanted. She talked about people and cats the same way, I thought.

"But surely even the cat's not going to keep on forever with something that's obviously not producing any results?"

"It will get tired of things after a while and find something else to do. But it sounds like she's pretty patient, so who knows. Maybe she'll manage to tame a stray."

"Or she might find another kitten to bring home with her," Yumiko said. I didn't pay much attention to her words at the time, but as it turned out this was precisely what happened. It occurred to me that Yumiko's tendency to discuss one possibility after another was somehow related to the fact that she had been living with cats too long.

"Not really. I think I've always been like this."

And that was more or less the end of our phone conversation that evening.

4

Starting sometime around the middle of July, Akira became obsessed with the idea of going to the beach.

Barring one or two days a month when something at the office made an eight-o'clock start unavoidable, I was not an early
riser. As a general rule I didn't get up until after ten, and I would
then spend a leisurely morning having breakfast, shaving, and all
the rest of it before setting out for work about an hour later. The
three other members of the ménage were all up hours before me.
Shimada left the house at eight every morning, and Yoko generally went out on the first of her feed-the-cats missions around the
same time. Akira sometimes went with her, and sometimes not—
but whether he went with her or stayed at home, he was still out
of bed and on his feet at roughly the same time. I had grown used
to enjoying the first hour or so of every day on my own. Akira's
beach obsession marked the end of my morning solitude.

The first thing I did every morning was go to the bathroom.
By the time I emerged less than a minute later, the curtains to my
room were drawn and Akira would be standing by the window
with a look on his face that made it clear he had something to say

that just couldn't wait. He'd give me a goofy grin and start singing at the top of his voice, his body gyrating in time to the "music."

> *Let's go once, let's go twice*
> *Let's all go to the seaside!*
> *Out in the fresh air, it's so nice,*
> *And the sea's so deep and wide!*

Every morning's performance was different, though the message of the song was always the same. One day he would make his pleas in the style of the Southern All-Stars, the next day it might come out as a kind of twisted homage to Elvis Costello or Liberace—though I was never able to guess who it was supposed to be until Akira told me.

He would accompany himself with improvised accessories: clutching my pillow to his chest and thrashing at it like a caveman guitarist, or sitting down intently at a chair in the kitchen and playing the breakfast table like a piano. I would listen to him wail and strut while I went about my morning routine, airing out my futon and wandering in and out of the room.

"You must have been practicing that Tom Waits impression all night," I said one morning.

"Are you kidding me? These performances are all one hundred percent genuine improvisations!"

Yoko shouted out her own contribution from the kitchen. "Whatever, Akira, I heard you humming that song while we were out walking this morning." But Akira was always happy so long as he was the focus of attention.

"That was yesterday's song. The Lou Reed one. That was pretty hot, huh?" Some days he'd seem to forget about his obsession for a while and would drop the subject of going to the beach once he'd delivered his daily song. Unfortunately, the Tom Waits morning was not one of these occasions.

> As the day dies and the sun slips like a drunk from his barstool
> Into an ocean of whiskey—
> And the clouds hang heavy in the sky like cigarette smoke
> And the sound of cocktail-hour thunder washes in from a
> piano across the bay—

Akira went on and on in his best Tom Waits style, but when Yoko called out that the coffee was ready I decided I'd had enough and went to join her in the kitchen.

"He really gets into that Tom Waits stuff, huh? Way more than when he's trying to do RC and things like that." The way she said it, ignoring any mention of the subject matter of Akira's daily improvisations, made me suspect that she didn't care one way or the other whether we went to the beach or not. What did she have against the shore?

"Oh, you know, it's always so crowded." This was a pretty obvious reason for not wanting to go to the beach, but it didn't sound that way when Yoko said it. "The beach is always full of people who only think of visiting the seaside in the summertime. Everywhere gets so packed. I don't think much of the people who come the rest of the year either. I mean, if they like it so much why not just live there all the time and save the effort, right? But those people who just come because it's summer or because it's what everyone else is doing—they're even worse than the worst of all."

I remembered that Yoko had grown up on the coast, and that the animosity she felt toward outsiders who spent their vacations there was a feeling common among people who lived in tourist destinations. But I was struck more by the words she had used. "Even worse than the worst of all." Was this just an awkward slip of the tongue—she was hardly the most eloquent of twenty-year-olds at the best of times—or had she chosen the words deliberately to emphasize how strongly she felt? If it was the latter, then it was clear that Yoko really didn't want to go to the beach. I was toying with these thoughts in my mind, spacing out and failing to give Yoko any kind of adequate reply, when Akira emerged from my room and clutched a chair to him as a microphone stand, swaying in time as he began to sing again.

> *The sun beats down on your head,*
> *Till you start to burn and your face gets so red,*
> *It's so hot, you're going to burn up your brains,*
> *Yay—ay-yay, hey hey,*
> *Your brains are gonna fry, and you're gonna lie . . .*
> *Down in the burning sun, a-huh-huh*

He was really straining his voice with this one. He brought his mouth close to the side of my face and screamed into my ear.

"All right, I get the message. Stop spitting on me."

"Really? We can go? When? When?"

He started spinning around the room, swinging the chair in the air. There was only one way out. I picked up my things and set off for the office.

That day I had a call from Mitani-san for the first time in several weeks, and set out to meet him at our usual coffee shop. As I walked down the stairs into the basement, I noticed a man with a deep tan and a shaved head waving at me from a table in the corner of the room. It was Mitani. He looked like someone who'd just been let out of jail, or a man about to embark on a pilgrimage. Either that or he was in some kind of avant-garde dance troupe. Even in the case of an easy-going middle-aged man like Mitani, a regular hairstyle made it much easier for people to feel at ease, I thought as I approached him. Come to think about it, no matter how laid-back a person looked, it was a rare individual who could get away with the shaved head look. "What's up with the hairdo, Baldie? Don't tell me you've renounced everything and decided to become a monk."

"Thanks for asking. Bali was a blast, man." No background, no explanatory preamble—just the bare bones and straight to the point. Typical Mitani.

But in his eyes there was none of the mad sparkle I was used to seeing whenever he unveiled the latest of his foolproof schemes for breaking the bank at the racetrack. His eyes looked vacant and unfocused, and his voice was flat when he spoke. Was this what a trip to Bali did to a man?

"I was there for a whole two weeks. Just got home the day before yesterday—or was it the day before that? Whatever." He said this with the air of a man who had forgotten to collect his brain from the airport luggage carousel.

Horse racing was the center of our friendship. It was the only thing we ever talked about—indeed, it was the only reason we ever met at all, and since mid-June I'd lost track of time since the races and meets were no longer there to mark off the days. It didn't make much difference whether we saw each other after a long interval or a short one—nothing out of the ordinary ever happened when we met anyway—and in the normal run of things it was difficult to remember each time I saw him when the last time had been.

My thoughts were interrupted by Mitani's latest pronouncement.

"I've just been chilling at home since I got back. Can't seem to find the energy for anything." He heaved a sigh that made it clear he wasn't joking—he seemed to have worn himself out just by coming out to the coffee shop to meet me. Mitani was rustling around for something in his bag.

"Here, I brought you this."

He pulled out a package of Balinese coffee and started to give me an explanation of how to drink it. The one thing you didn't do with this stuff, apparently, was strain it through a filter. Instead you added hot water directly to the grounds, and then let the dregs sink to the bottom. You drank the coffee on top and left the grounds at the bottom. Probably part of the reason it tasted so good, Mitani-san said, was that when you drank the coffee in Bali they served it in a glass instead of a cup, so that you could see the dregs at the bottom of the glass. That way you avoided getting a mouthful of muck when you got to the bottom of the glass. "I tell you, when you drink this stuff over there, it's like you're flying, man." I could hardly hear what he was saying thanks to the so-called background music. The music had changed from the last time we'd been here two or three weeks ago. Now they were playing something loud by a Japanese rock band I didn't recognize.

I couldn't even remember what kind of music they played here before. That's the whole point of background music, I guess—once you start to notice it, it's not doing its job. But until now there had always been something unobtrusive playing softly, and the place was always full of people like Mitani and me, chatting quietly to each other. The fact that the music had changed must mean that the management was looking to attract a younger crowd—once that happened, we'd have to start looking for a new place to meet. Mitani was still babbling away about his trip, and when I emerged from my reverie I found he was telling me about a festival he'd been to in Bali.

The ceremony had been held in a semi-secret location—a village in the middle of nowhere, apparently—and without the right connections, you had no chance of finding it. It wasn't like a festival in Japan, where anyone and his dog could turn up unannounced. This was something on a totally different level from the tedious festivals that the respectable scholarly groups went to at the invitation of the Indonesian government. Mitani started to pull photos out of his bag as he described what he'd seen.

The main focus of the occasion seemed to be the trance-like state entered into by a number of the villagers. Mitani's photos showed the ceremony leading up to the trance, then there was some kind of dance with masks, followed by a witch doctor and some other character doing something mysterious with sticks; and then, just as the main festivities were about to begin, a torrential downpour of tropical rain. After the rain stopped, it was time for the trances.

"Once they go into the trance, they stick these metal spikes in them. Like this, look. Big, thick skewers. And they don't feel a thing. Not a thing. And then one of the spike guys takes the spike out and turns to face the audience—and starts making like he's going to stick them into us. It's pretty wild. He's waving these spikes around in the air and lunging at people. Scared the shit out of me, man. Look, I couldn't even hold my camera properly."

Just as he had said, not a single one of all the pictures documenting this stage of the proceedings gave a decent impression of what was happening—they were blurred by camera shake, or showed a person's face that took up half the frame, or nothing but sky. It was hard to get a clear impression of the scene as a whole, but the expression on Mitani's face and the way he talked gave me some idea of what had gone down.

"Obviously, it's only the young guys who can do that. Some of the old guys were telling stories about how they used to do it too back in the day, and some of them kind of pretend that they're going into a trance even now. But the old guys don't do any of that shit with the spikes, man. They're not even allowed near the spikes anymore. Oh yeah, look at this one. What do you think about that? Look: this guy's putting a chicken in his mouth. This is something even the old guys can still do. That's a real live chicken. Look, its head is right inside his mouth. And it's flapping its wings right in his face. And then in the end, he eats it. A live fucking chicken.

"But you could tell his eyes weren't really gone. Every now and then you saw him looking around the place, like he was checking to see that everyone's still watching. And all the time this fucking chicken's going nuts right in front of his nose. What a dude.

"Oh yeah, and then look at this guy. Shit—I guess that one didn't come out. What about this one? Dammit, the fucker turned his back on me.

"I tell you, this guy was totally gone. His eyes were totally glazed, his pupils dilated. Then all of a sudden he turns and comes lunging straight at me. I was scared shitless, man. I tell you, you don't want to end up at the front of that crowd.

"The villagers, you could tell they kind of knew somehow when the guy was going to come at them. That's the only explanation I can think of. Suddenly they'd all just kind of shuffle off to the back.

"So if you don't keep your wits about you, if you switch off for even one second, you're gonna get left on your own at the front. Then this guy with the spike, he starts lunging in a different direction. And everyone rushes back to where they were standing before. It's like a sixth sense or something. And they stand there watching all this with their arms folded. I mean, if you're at the back there's this wall of people in front of you, but once the guy gets close it's another story. No way I could take decent pictures with shit like that going on around me."

Mitani went on and on with his stories. Eventually we moved away from the festival and onto landscape shots of beaches and temples. But Mitani wasn't very good at explaining things, and I hardly understood a word of what he was trying to tell me. I restricted myself to occasional murmured interjections, and the next thing I knew he had moved on to some kind of special massage technique that a Balinese shaman had shown him—a technique that Mitani said (this was more like his usual self now) was guaranteed to drive women wild. He went on in this vein for a while, with me half-listening and half-understanding what he said.

And then suddenly he wasn't talking about this magic sexual technique anymore, and he heaved a heavy sigh as if he'd worn himself out by talking at such length. "I don't think I'll bother going in to work today. I'm going home. See you around." He left the coffee shop and walked back in the direction of the station.

There was still no end to Akira's morning assaults of self-composed songs on the "Let's Go to the Beach" theme. If anything, they were growing more ferocious by the day. He clearly wasn't going to rest until his wish came true.

Every morning I ate my breakfast surrounded by noise and chaos. The guy wouldn't give up. It was the spitting in my face that got to me the most. I made the mistake of complaining to him about this, but this only encouraged him to add spittle-flecked phrases to his performance wherever he could fit them in. "Pa, pa, pa, the ss-eaaa-sside." I raised my fist and made ready to hit him, but he just jumped back a couple of paces and went right on singing. As soon as I started eating again he was back at my side, shouting into my ear. "Let's go, let's go, let's go go go!" Another shower of spittle. "All right," I told him, "I give up—we'll go." But Akira wasn't about to be put off by such a noncommittal promise. "When are we going to go, when are we going to go, when when

when when when?!" It sounded as though it might never stop. I'd had enough of Akira and his antics. I looked over at Yoko for moral support, but she was calmly sipping her coffee or occasionally getting up to check on the laundry, and didn't notice what was going on at all. When it came time to hang the clothes to dry, Akira suddenly stopped singing and darted over to help. I had to laugh. This was my chance. I got up to leave (it was really more like an escape), and called out a quick "See you later" as I closed the door. But Akira came running after me, and shouted out after me from the door. "I'll find us a driver!" It was his parting shot.

As a result of all this fuss I ended up leaving for work slightly earlier than usual. Tokyo is a city with lots of green in the center of town, and lots more around the edges—but not much in between. Downtown areas around the Imperial Palace and the Meiji Shrine are full of huge soaring trees, but as you move out from the center the patches of green among the steel and concrete become ever more sporadic. By the time you get out as far as somewhere like Nakamurabashi, though, you're surrounded by trees again everywhere you go, many of them untamed by municipal pruning shears. On mornings when I had a bit of time to spare, I liked to take a roundabout way to the station and enjoyed walking among the trees, impressed anew by just how much nature there still was in the city if you had the time to find it.

You notice the wind much more when there are trees around. You can see at a glance whether there is any wind, and how strong it is. You might feel the heat even more than usual on days when there isn't much wind—but the shade of the trees was preferable to a bit of a breeze in the heart of the city, where there is nothing but buildings and concrete and hardly a tree in sight—and walking through the trees at ten or eleven in the morning filled me with a sense of well-being and oneness with nature. Even the sticky dampness under my shirt didn't bother me. It was just another part of nature. What could be more natural than a bit of sweat?

Another thing that appealed to me about walking to the station the long way was that I thought I'd be more likely to bump into Mew and Miao again. Yoko had seen them two or three times since the day we'd first spotted them together, but that wasn't good enough for me—I wanted to see with my own eyes what the two kittens looked like now. And lo and behold, I did see them again that day—in a spot I'd never really looked before. I guess this makes sense. A cat is not a tree, and you're not going to have much luck if you're always looking in the same place.

The two cats were sitting side by side in the middle of a series of steps that led up to an apartment building on the other side of the road, just three or four lots down from where I'd seen them before. They were sitting in the shade of a roof just above head level. A slight breeze coming through the open slats at the back of the steps made it the perfect spot to sit and watch the world go by. They were in no hurry to leave, and sat calmly as I stopped to watch them.

Now that I saw their faces next to one another I realized that Miao—the more cautious, timid one of the pair—had a slightly bigger patch of white around his nose. Even so, I couldn't be sure whether it had been Mew or Miao that had paid me that first visit back in the winter. As I stood and watched them, memories of that long-gone winter's day came back to me vividly. There are moments in life when buried memories come surging up to the surface of consciousness, and you have the sensation that you're in two places at once. It is the kind of experience that can freeze you to the spot—or at least make you want to stand rooted to the ground as long as the feeling lasts. I stood in silence until suddenly there came the sound of someone opening a door up on the second floor.

Mew and Miao shot off at the sound, springing up from where they'd been sitting and disappearing through the gaps between the steps. They were such grown-up cats now. They seemed to have fled for good, and I knew they probably wouldn't show their faces again for a while. The woman who lived in the apartment on the second floor seemed to be waiting for me to turn and walk away. As I did so, I heard the sound of her footsteps coming down the stairs.

I was changing trains at Shibuya when I bumped into Mitani as I passed through the ticket gate. He gave me a look of despair that told me he'd had enough of work for today already, before the day had even started. "It's so hot," he gasped. The heat was stifling, like a heavy blanket draped over the city. There was dust everywhere. Why not stop off for something to drink first, Mitani suggested. I couldn't think of any reason to refuse. We passed out through the ticket gates again and made our way in silence across a footbridge over the main road toward a coffee shop on the opposite side of a crowded roundabout. It was only once we were sitting down that he spoke. "So, how you been?" Apparently he still hadn't made it into the office since his return from Bali—this was laid-back even by Mitani's standards—but this wasn't what he wanted to talk about, to judge from the next thing he said, which had nothing to do with work or practical life whatsoever.

"Tell me—what do you know about Kabbalah," he said. Kabbalah, black magic, mumbo-jumbo—I knew nothing about these things beyond the words themselves. On subjects like these the only contribution I was capable of were non-words like "um," "ah" and "uh-huh." They were barely even sounds, really. But for Mitani this was good enough. He intended to take things in his own time, as he always did.

"There's this guy in Kobe who writes books about it," he said. "They say he uses Kabbalah to insert himself into books and tarot cards. Thing is, he's really nearsighted, so he can hardly see what's around him. I've never met him, but what do you think? It could be true, right? Everyone says so." As with his claims that the results of every horse race in Japan were fixed, there was no proof for what he had said beyond the fact that Mitani had just said it—whether "everyone" was saying it or just one specific individual made no difference. But it would have been stupid to expect proof from Mitani. He'd warmed to his subject now, and there was excitement in his voice as he continued.

"He went over to England for a year to study the Kabbalah. By this stage he's in his fifties—married with kids. He leaves everything behind in Japan, and goes off on his own. And that's where things start to get interesting. Personally, I believe what he says. Apparently, it *is* possible to make your dreams come true. The important thing is: No doubts. You have to stay focused, and keep on believing." So there was nothing more to it than positive thinking?

"You kidding? There're serious techniques involved. Otherwise, it wouldn't be Kabbalah, right? The occult is all about proper practice and technique. I couldn't tell you how it works. I don't know all the details yet. You think I'd waste my time sitting here with you if I knew all that?"

Presumably he'd be off putting his special skills to some magical use. But you couldn't take these things too seriously when you were talking to Mitani.

"You never know how long you're going to have to wait. And how much will cost you. You don't know what you'll have to give up to get what you want. Sometimes you'll lose it first, other times you don't lose anything till long after your wish has come true. It's only once it's over that you can look back and understand.

"Anyway, this guy I was talking about. He's been in England for six months or so, and there's one book he can't find anywhere. Some book written in the eighteenth century, and without it there are aspects of the whole thing that he just can't figure out.

"So he uses Kabbalah. And what do you know—along comes the book. This book he's been searching for everywhere. Turns up in a used bookstore somewhere for next to nothing. He looks inside and there's no doubt about it—it's the real thing. He's over the moon, right? So he buys the book and takes it home. And when he gets home he realizes that his gold watch has been stolen—an old family heirloom, worth a fortune. Someone must have stolen it while he was in the bookstore. That was the price he had to pay to get what he wanted. Come to think of it, though, what was he doing walking around wearing such a priceless watch in the first place, right?" Mitani said with a laugh.

"Maybe it was like bait—so that he'd be able to get his hands on that book."

"It happens. Maybe it was unconscious, but the power of the Kabbalah made him do it," Mitani replied, apparently quite serious.

"The next thing that happened was his travel bag gets stolen. Cash, passport, travelers checks—everything. Not a guy to take much care of his belongings, I guess. But a lot of them are like that—they're so fixated on the mystical side of things that they're a bit vague about everyday stuff.

"Anyway, it's nearly time for him to come back to Japan, and he hasn't got a cent. So what does he do? He uses Kabbalah again. This time, he gets news from home about a week later, telling him that his house has been completely destroyed in a fire. He has a hunch that something's about to happen, and sure enough, his insurance comes through and a big chunk of money arrives from Japan. So that's the way it works—your wishes will definitely come true, but you never know what price you'll have to pay."

Mitani took a deep breath and heaved a sigh—which I took to mean that he'd finished. But so far all the talk had been about this mysterious Kabbalist. We hadn't discussed Mitani himself at all yet. The conversation seemed to be at an end, but something gave me the feeling that there was more to come.

"The next step for him was to enter into the very highest levels of Kabbalah," Mitani continued quietly. There was something different in his voice now. He told me that in order to attain this highest level of expertise in the dark arts, a person had to give up the thing that was more precious to him than anything else in the world. What did I think that was, Mitani asked suddenly.

It was typical of Mitani. He'd be chatting at his own pace while I sat back and added nothing but the occasional nod, and then—out of nowhere—he'd throw me a question out of left field. In the circumstances, the only answer I could come up with was pretty lame. "His eyesight?"

Mitani came straight back with his theory. He had already reached his own conclusion, and no other answer could possibly exist. "I think it's his fame, his reputation. Everyone's going to forget about him."

But if everyone forgot him there would be no one around to check up on his achievements—there would be no such thing as truth or lies anymore as far as the man and his magic were concerned. These mystics have got it all worked out. But Mitani wasn't finished.

"Even if that happens, I won't forget him. Someday, I'll meet him." With this, Mitani finally brought everything he had said until now back round to himself. I don't know if you could call this attitude of Mitani's an optimistic view of the world—the habit he had of suggesting that he alone had found a way to ensure that he would monopolize happiness—but after this remark he laughed happily and gave me his usual farewell. "Be seein' ya." And he was off.

We hadn't talked about horses once—not today, and not the previous time, either. Maybe Mitani's enthusiasm for horses had started to cool since his Bali trip. Or maybe he was still working hard to find a connection between horse racing and the occult. Yes—knowing Mitani, that was by far the likelier explanation.

As I mentioned earlier, the horse racing season had tailed off a bit since June—there weren't as many races in the summer, so that without a regular procession of races to attend, things became a blur and time tended to lag when Ishigami and I did get together. At the start of August he suddenly announced that he was going on a trip to England for work.

I struggled to remember what it was he did for a living. Certainly I couldn't picture him doing the kind of job that would require business trips to the other side of the world. Ishigami apparently felt the same way himself.

"I know. I never thought my work would take me to England either, to tell you the truth," he said as he sipped at his beer, talking about his job as if it had nothing to do with him at all. "You really want to know?" he asked, and then went on sipping at his beer as if to say that I didn't really need to know at all. I was starting to think that I could live without knowing, when he suddenly embarked on an explanation in an unusually businesslike tone of voice.

"It's not a big deal or anything, really," he said. Apparently he was shooting some kind of prospectus video for a girls' high school, and they were following some of the students on a school trip to England to shoot footage for the video. Ishigami had been asked to go along and help out. Once this rather banal explanation was out of the way he began to warm to his subject and continued in his usual tone of voice.

"It's a sign of the times, is what it is," he said, pausing to create a silence in which I was supposed to meditate on the wisdom of his words.

"In my day, it would have been unthinkable for a bunch of high school kids to go off around the world like that. We didn't have the same freedom back then. Overseas travel was a privilege, not a right."

All this talk of freedom was just like Ishigami. I smiled wryly to myself, but there was no stopping him now.

"Listen—I'm serious. It's the same thing with imported fruit. Bananas from Taiwan, oranges from God knows where. It's a part of ordinary life now, but it wasn't always like that. Kids today, they think everything's always been the way it is now.

"Remember how expensive imported records were back in our day? But these kids don't give a shit about any of that stuff. They don't know how lucky they are."

This was one of Ishigami's favorite themes, but it was clear from his laugh that he didn't really care much one way or the other. Then he roused himself and started to talk energetically again.

"Even these kids don't have it all their own way. They have to go in their school uniforms! Ha! Fucking hilarious, man." Ishigami laughed like a donkey, as though it were the most gratifyingly ridiculous thing he'd heard in a long time. Personally, I couldn't help thinking that the presence of Ishigami and the rest of his crew might have had something to do with it. The idea that you had to dress up to look your best on TV sounded like something out of the '50s to me. Ishigami looked me straight in the eye and swallowed heavily, waving his hand vigorously in the air in disagreement.

"You're wrong," he said. "They wore their uniforms last year too. And the year before that. Actually, it's only until they get there that they have to wear their uniforms. But they're definitely in their little sailor suits all the time they're on the plane. God knows what all the foreigners on the plane are going to think. They'll probably think it's some Girl Scouts division of the Navy or something. Or what if they think the war's starting up again? The Falklands all over again." Ishigami breathed a sigh and ordered a gin to chase his beer.

It occurred to me that Ishigami was thirty-four now, and the girls he'd be traveling with would be just seventeen or eighteen. In terms of age, they were more like father and daughter than brother and sister. The news that they would be boarding a plane in their sailor-suit school uniforms set him off on one of his riffs about international trade and the freedom of travel in the modern age, and jokes about an outbreak of war. Ishigami wasn't normally given to introspection or thinking about subjects such as the generation gap—but put him together with a bunch of schoolgirls who were even less interested in it than he was, and he suddenly found himself acting like a member of the older generation whether he liked it or not. There was something tragicomical about it. Even the idea of listening to Ishigami spouting about these things struck me as faintly ridiculous.

After a while our conversation moved onto horse racing, and Ishigami pulled a paperback edition of a Dick Francis novel from his bag.

"Japan's still cut off from the rest of the world as far as racing is concerned," he said. I didn't need Ishigami to tell me this—but the idea of Japan being somehow isolated from the rest of the world made me suspect that he was about to launch into another dissertation on his freedom theme.

"Things are different overseas," he said. "The horse's owner might be from France, the trainer's an American, and the jockey's English. Arab princes buying horses from French owners." The way he said it (and the look he gave me after he'd said it) reminded me of the cocky look you see on the faces of drunks when they've just delivered a particularly pithy piece of advice. And once again, I hadn't needed Ishigami to tell me this; it was nothing I didn't already know. But what did it matter? There was no rule that said a conversation had to consist of entirely new information, and so long as both partners were interested in hearing the old stuff again then what was the harm in a bit of innocent repetition?

"Is there anywhere in Japan where you can buy maps or guides to the racecourses of England?" I asked. Ishigami pointed his index finger at me and shook his head vigorously from side to side.

"You must be joking. As if they'd sell stuff like that here. That's one of the things about reading Dick Francis books. If you read Dick Francis, you find out where most of the racecourses in England are. It's the only way to find out, really. Most of the action happens at racecourses, but a lot of the time you've only a vague idea where the places are. Such and such a course is near London; this track is so many miles north or south of Liverpool, whatever. They like to give you all the details in these foreign books."

"If you really want to know, why not just buy a map? You can look up places like Epsom and Ascot easily enough, right? I mean, they're just place names, after all."

"I already did," Ishigami replied, giving me that self-satisfied drunken look again. Fair enough. But then, his job involved making plans and traveling around all the time, so it was no surprise that he was practical-minded and good at finding things out. Or so I thought. His next words made me reconsider. "They're not there," he said. Apparently none of the famous racetracks were anywhere on his map.

"I mean, I found Ascot easily enough—the town, I mean. But there's no racecourse. And it's a pretty big map; all the museums and galleries are there. But no racecourse. How can that be?

"I mean, if that's all they're going to tell you, you'd be better off reading Dick Francis and using your imagination." But the way he said it made it clear that such things didn't matter much in the end. I agreed that he was right (what else could I say?) and we started to chat in a vague way about what we thought might happen at some of the upcoming races.

But as it happened there weren't really any major races coming up—only minor affairs, and neither of us could work up much enthusiasm about those—and our conversation wandered forward to the season proper that would start up again in September and back to the Derby we'd seen two months earlier.

We moved on for a few more drinks somewhere else, and before we went our separate ways at the end of the evening Ishigami made me a promise. "I'll bring you back a horseshoe from Epsom," he said, before he staggered into a taxi and disappeared into the night.

Akira and Yoko had been at the center of my home life for most of the summer. On the day that Gonta moved in I left work a little earlier than usual and arrived back at Nakamurabashi station around five thirty in the evening. It wasn't that I'd managed to finish everything I needed to do particularly early or anything—but it was such a nice summer's day that I found it impossible to get into the mood for work. I decided that resistance was useless, and packed up and left the office early.

It's still as bright as noon at five thirty in July, even though by seven—just ninety minutes later—it's already getting dark. Arriving home in daylight always made me feel as though I still had half the day to look forward to, and I walked home from the station with a spring in my step.

Akira jumped out at me as I opened the door to the apartment. He seemed to have been waiting for his moment to pounce. "Guess what, guess what, guess what," he said. Had something happened? I didn't want to encourage him, so I kept my voice as flat as I possibly could. "What is it?"

"I found us a driver! To take us to the beach!" As he spoke, he dragged out from behind him a guy around his own age, who was slightly smaller than himself. Next to Akira, he looked almost presentable. "This is Gonta," Akira said.

Gonta beamed a smile and bowed his head in my direction. Unusual for a young man in his early twenties, Gonta didn't come across as awkward or introverted at all, and there was none of the aggressiveness that a lot of people his age display when meeting someone older for the first time. That kind of attitude always elicits a response in me—I was glad to see that this wasn't going to be a problem with Gonta.

"Gonta makes films too," Akira said. He seemed to want to tell me his friend's life story all at once. What was I supposed to say to a remark like this? I looked over at Gonta. "Really?" I said, and then went into the next room to get changed.

Akira followed behind me, talking to Gonta as he did so. "See, he doesn't even bother to ask what kind of films you make. Doesn't even say he'd like to see them some time, or anything." Akira was really making an effort to turn on the charm tonight.

"What kind of films do you make? I'll love to see 'em some time," I parroted back at him. Gonta glanced at Akira and burst out laughing. "Gonta's always making films, but he's never once actually finished one," Akira said. "But they're pretty good anyway." I changed into fresh clothes and went to the bathroom to wash up and rinse my mouth.

"He shoots on 8mm video. But he gets pretty pissed if you try to tell him he's not making a film but just shooting a video," Akira babbled happily.

"What does it matter," I shouted back from the bathroom. "If the guy making it says it's a film, that's good enough for me."

Gonta had hardly said a word since I got home, but somehow I knew that this wasn't a sign that he was particularly shy or introverted or (worst of all) that he could never find a word to say to anyone more than five years older than him. He was just being polite—we'd only just met, after all—and although he wasn't saying very much, the beaming smile that never seemed to leave his face was almost capable of holding up one end of a conversation on its own.

"He takes this little 8mm camera with him wherever he goes. And he starts filming just when you least expect it—talking to himself the whole time. Weird, or what?

"When I'm with him I try to keep quiet. I don't want to talk when he's filming. But he tells me to just let it all out—you know, be normal.

"But the stuff he films—I can't follow it at all. If it was just Gonta talking to himself, it might just about hold together. But the people with him change from scene to scene. None of it makes any sense."

A film that contained the voices of random people coming in at unpredictable moments was obviously going to lack something in terms of consistency and unity of theme. Akira was probably just showing off that he knew a thing or two about proper filmmaking techniques. He had hardly paused to draw breath. Suddenly he stopped and looked at us seriously and sighed through his nose.

"What the fuck? Now I'm the one talking to myself. No one else has said a word since you got home." He scratched his head in mock confusion, like something out of a stage comedy, then turned his attentions back to himself again.

"Quit staring at me like that, you guys. Look, I'm blushing. Come on, Gonta—say something." I think Akira was worried that I was going to dismiss his friend as an idiot if he stood there in silence much longer. Gonta said nothing for a few seconds. He seemed to be thinking of something to say.

"Would it be all right if I talked about something other than my films?" he said with a smile. Now that he mentioned it I realized that Akira had been talking about nothing else since I'd arrived home, even though no one (and certainly not Gonta himself) had shown any interest in the subject.

"Do you not like talking about your own work?" I asked—at least partly out of politeness—I was more than ready to move onto another topic of conversation myself by this stage. "Or do you just feel that Akira's making fun of you when he talks like that?"

"Well, that's just the way Akira is, and I don't think anyone takes what he says too seriously. It's just that when I meet someone for the first time, I'd rather talk about other stuff, you know. Just normal chitchat, you know."

I certainly did. In fact, I liked nothing better. But as it happened, the chitchat failed to materialize, and for a few moments we sat in silence.

"Oh great," Akira said. "I know: Why don't you two just sit here and stare at each other in silence and I'll go off and talk to myself. I know when I'm not wanted." This sounded like just the kind of meaningless conversation we'd been looking for. I looked from Akira to Gonta, and saw that Gonta was looking back and forth between Akira and me. We both broke up laughing.

"What surprises me," I said, "is that Akira knows anyone with a driver's license. I didn't think that was his crowd."

"It's true that most of us can't drive. A lot of people who are into films tend to spend all their money on that. It can get inconvenient at times. I decided to get my own license so I wouldn't have to depend on anyone else."

"So you do have some money, then?" I said. It was as though my lips were moving instinctively in response to what he'd said. Akira burst out laughing, and Gonta replied with an embarrassed grin.

"Not really. Like, money—what's that, right? I may have a license, but I certainly don't own a car."

"Are you serious? Hey, what kind of driver is this you've found us, Akira? A rental car driver? That doesn't count!"

Akira muttered something to himself under his breath. I felt an urge to make him sweat a little more.

"Listen, Akira: I'm not spending any money on this trip of yours, so if you think I'm going to go out and hire a car for you, think again. It's time you came to terms with the consequences of the way you live your life. You're the one who's got no money. Take the fucking train if you're so desperate to go—if you can even afford that. Wait, wait—I know what you're going to say. *But it's no fun going to the beach unless you go by car.* Yeah right. You're such a shit sometimes, Akira, you know that? What are you afraid of? *Ah, ah, ah! It's so hot! The sun's beating down on my poor head! This heat is killing me!* Good—fuck off and die for all I care."

Gonta seemed to enjoy the performance. He obviously knew how things got after a while when you spent time with Akira. Akira himself looked up at me sheepishly. "You don't really mind, do you?" This made me want to give him another dose of the same, but luckily for him Yoko came floating into the room just as I was getting ready to let rip.

Yoko had a large plastic shopping bag in her hand. "Who knew cat food could get so heavy? I guess anything can make you break a sweat if you buy enough of it," she said. She set the shopping bag on the floor and took a gauze handkerchief from her pocket, which she proceeded to dab at her nose and forehead before using it to wipe the sweat from her neck and then plunging her hand straight down inside her bright red tank-top to deal with things down there. Her movements were natural and relaxed, but even so I felt slightly embarrassed when her hand went inside her shirt. Yoko didn't seem to notice or care.

"So I was going around putting out food for the cats after lunch this afternoon. And the stuff that was still left there from yesterday had already gone bad and was giving off this really funky smell.

It's this heat. I guess you can't leave canned food sitting around outside in this heat and expect it to stay fresh.

"So I decided to switch to dry food. And what's even better is that dry food is way cheaper," Yoko said to no one in particular as she filed the boxes of dry food away in the place where the cans of cat food were normally kept. I looked over at Gonta and noticed that he had taken out his video camera and was filming Yoko as she put the cat food away. In less time than it took me to turn around, he was pointing the thing at me.

"See, what did I tell you," Akira said. "Always filming stuff before you know it."

I had to laugh. Akira himself had spent most of his time since moving into my apartment taking pictures of Yoko without so much as a by-your-leave, and now here he was criticizing Gonta for doing the same thing. I was going to have a go at him for it. *You're always turning a blind eye to your own behavior and pointing the finger at other people*—but I decided to say nothing and enjoy my own laughter. I noticed that Gonta was no longer zooming in on me—probably because I was laughing like an idiot—and was now filming the three of us together.

With a photo, there's a click of the shutter and it's all over. Not so with a video camera. Gonta's film just kept on rolling. There were four of us in the room. Three of us were laughing and being laughed at in turn—chatting about nothing and thinking about cats—while one person stood on his own with an unchanging expression and a camera that kept on filming. It was weird. There was something odd about the things he was filming too, and I decided to speak up and ask him what he was doing.

"Whenever someone's actually doing something—like me laughing just now, or Yoko putting away the cat food—your camera never seems to follow them. I mean, normally, you'd expect someone to film what people are doing, but that's not what you're looking for, is it? You seem to let the camera move from place to place almost at random."

My eyes seemed to be drawn in by Gonta's camera, and I realized as I spoke that I was following the track of his lens as it followed the three of us around the room. I couldn't help noticing the movement of my eyes as they flitted from one to another of my companions. Gonta kept right on filming as he replied.

"This takes practice. The whole time the film's rolling I'm watching what's going on through the view-finder, right? But if I'm negligent or—not negligent, but if I'm not careful and I let my concentration lapse—then the camera moves automatically to the person who's talking or whoever's moving around the most or whatever. Weird, no?"

He paused for a few seconds, trying to find the right words for what he wanted to say next, but the camera kept on moving. As I watched, I could almost believe him what he said about this being the result of extensive training.

"The thing is, as long as I do it like this, what I come up with is not going to turn into a film—well, not a normal film, anyway. I mean, in normal films the camera concentrates on the person who's talking, right? But while that person's talking you don't get to see the person they're talking to, right? A lot of the time when two people are talking to each other, often the listener isn't looking at the person who's talking at all. They might be looking down at the ground or up at the ceiling. It's not much fun if you're the one talking, though, and the other person won't look at least vaguely in your direction. I mean, no one wants to talk to someone wearing dark sunglasses, right?"

I was impressed by what he was saying, and suddenly heard myself interrupting in a loud voice that I thought Gonta was "amazing." No one reacted much, and they certainly didn't look surprised or anything; everyone just carried on as if nothing had happened. I felt I ought to clarify what I had meant. "Most people who make films would never think of things like that."

"Well, praise is always nice, obviously," Gonta said with a smile, his camera still turning. "It was while I was filming that it came to me."

"That's great," I said. "That's what's so amazing about it." Such a rapid-fire succession of "greats" and "amazings" sounded over the top even to me. Gonta carried on calmly and quietly with what he was doing.

"This is the first time I've ever discussed it with anyone. I mean, I always have these thoughts running through my mind when I'm filming, and sometimes I speak my thoughts out loud to myself as I work—but this is the first time I've ever talked about it with anyone but . . . myself, I guess. Somehow you just come to understand—or feel—things like this if you spend long enough making films."

"That's fantastic. It's as though your brain and your camera are united as one when you work," I said, letting my eyes move from one person to another around me just like Gonta's camera.

"But you can't imagine what the films are like till you actually see them," Akira said. He sounded almost jealous.

"Whatever, Akira. You were the one who started off saying how interesting you thought Gonta's films were.

"I'm really impressed by your ideas and your whole approach, Gonta. Not many filmmakers start out from that kind of perspective. Most of them are just interested in shooting a story. But Gonta's interested in other things: What makes a story interesting? What does it mean to live in a world where cameras are present? Stuff like that.

"So even if what he's filming now turns out to be dull or uninteresting, it doesn't really matter. Sooner or later he'll shoot a completely different kind of film. Well, there's always the possibility, anyway."

I tailed off a bit towards the end. As I listened to the sound of my own voice, what I was saying struck me as sounding a bit over the top. Akira pointed to himself. "What about me then?"

"*What about me, then?* Listen to you," I said. "Always talking about nothing but yourself. Don't worry, Akira: You're just fine. Hunky-dory. A wunderkind of the mundane. A genius of the banal." Uncertain how to react, Akira cracked up, but then looked up at me with a twinkle in his eye. "Is that good? Or are you making fun of me again?"

"Don't worry about it, Akira. You're a marvel, a real rarity. In your case, criticism and praise come to the same thing. So don't worry about it, you're all right."

After that, we took it easy for a while, shooting the breeze and drinking beer, until Yoko decided she'd rather go back into the kitchen and see to the dry cat food she'd brought home. She sat on the floor poring over the ingredients and contents information printed on the side of each box, and after a while we heard the unmistakable sound of crunching and chewing. We'd been standing there half-watching what she was doing, and now that she'd started eating all three of us turned to look at each other in amazement.

"You're really going to eat that?" Akira shouted in amazement. Yoko looked surprised.

"Hey, this stuff isn't bad, you know," she said, as if there were nothing out of the ordinary in what she was doing.

"You can't eat that."

"Why not? Am I going to turn into a cat?"

"How do you even know if it's safe to eat?"

"Whatever. It's not like it's got poison in it or anything. I thought I should at least taste it to check the flavor before I gave any of it to the cats."

"Oh, come on—nnn," Akira said. He looked over at me as though asking for moral support, but I was too taken aback by the thought that had just crossed my mind.

"Does that mean you tried the canned stuff too?" I asked.

"Of course," she replied.

I was impressed. Akira was looking at me with an unhappy and troubled smile on his face. He didn't know what to make of this at all.

"But . . ."

"Yoko's right, Akira. What's the big deal?"

"But . . ."

This time Akira turned to Gonta for support, but Gonta was just smiling to himself with that inscrutable "Gonta look" on his face. "Today's a day for thinking outside the box," I blurted, still suffering the aftereffects of my earlier bout of overexcitement. I was pretty much talking out loud to myself. Even so, it was nice to have people around to hear what I was saying. How *fun* everything is this evening, I thought.

After a while Yoko announced that she was going to pop out and distribute some cat food, and started pulling out empty plastic and Tupperware containers from under the sink. It was still light out and I was feeling in such a good mood that I decided to go with her. Gonta and Akira agreed to come too (not that anyone had asked them), and the four of us set out together to follow Yoko on her rounds.

We all settled down to Yoko's pace as soon as we started walking. It was Yoko who was in charge of the group—not so much of the speed at which we walked as the mood in which we did it. Yoko generally walked more or less in the middle of the road, her eyes constantly flitting about in search of cats—in the gaps between fences, on rooftops, and in the branches of trees. Akira and Gonta took turns walking ahead or bringing up the rear on either side of her. We were like a family of cats ourselves: Yoko the mother cat led the way, and the three of us followed behind her like little kittens.

Yoko seemed to avoid leaving the cat food on private property, instead choosing parking lots, empty spaces, and allotments planted with cabbages. She buried any leftovers first, then put the empty container into the plastic bag she had brought with her.

"Up till now I've been putting food out in fifteen places, but with the dry food it should be less effort so I can start leaving it in more places from now on."

There must have been no small effort involved in burying left-over food and dealing with the packaging every day—so the switch to dry food would make things easier for her personally too. Yoko ducked down an alleyway between two houses and changed the food there. "Akira saw one here recently. A little white one, with a pattern on his tail. Ever since then I've been leaving some food for him here."

Akira was clicking away with his camera as she talked. "I love the way her face looks when she's saying nice things about me," he said. Whether she had really meant to praise him or not by admitting that he'd spotted one of the neighborhood cats I didn't know—but there was no doubting that Akira's mood and his reaction to things were closely linked with his camera. Perhaps Gonta wasn't the only one who interacted with the world through a lens.

Just then, a black cat with white paws marched proudly and serenely across the road a few meters in front of where we were standing.

"Don't you think he looks like a mischievous one?" Yoko said. Apparently the cat was a notorious neighborhood nuisance. It had pissed on a futon that someone had hung out to dry, causing the owner of the futon to post an angry notice that read: *Please stop feeding the black cat that has been prowling the neighborhood.*

"But the notice was kind of weird, actually," Yoko said. I mean, there was a little picture of the cat on the sign, and he looked so cute. He didn't look like a bad cat at all. Just a bit cheeky. Actually, I think whoever made the sign probably likes cats too. Probably they'd feed Blackie themselves if they could—but they're still kind of ticked off about the futon I guess."

So she had taken to calling this one Blackie. No surprises there.

Akira didn't take more than four or five pictures the whole time we were out walking. Since he came out on this walk twelve or thirteen times a week with Yoko, I guess he couldn't afford to be too snap-happy every time he covered the same ground. But for Gonta, this was all new, and his camera was rolling the whole time, shooting footage of the three of us as we walked, and of the Nakamurabashi area itself—the scattered apartment buildings surrounded by fields that still took up most of the area, a few old farm houses surviving here and there with their thatched roofs, several grand old houses with gardens full of ancient trees penned in by fences—turning the camera at regular intervals toward the sky as the sun slipped toward the horizon. What he was capturing on film was not the details themselves so much as the overall experience.

It felt good to spend time together like this as the summer evening turned into night. It felt good to be here now, in this place and in this moment. Yoko was right—what need was there to go all the way to the beach or anywhere else for that matter, when one had such simple pleasures so close at hand every day? But as I was thinking these thoughts, Yoko herself—perhaps prompted by a similar train of thought—arrived at precisely the opposite conclusion, and announced that she wouldn't mind going to the beach after all.

It was around eight thirty when we got back to the apartment, so we must have been out walking for about two hours. Shimada was home from work by the time we got back, and was slumped in a chair dressed only in an undershirt. The summer heat had prompted even him to take off his shirt for a change.

The sight of him stripped down to just a T-shirt brought home to me just how emaciated and weak he was. He looked like an old man. You couldn't help wishing he'd put his shirt back on so that you could relax. I did my best to ignore his appearance, and was introducing him to Gonta when he interrupted me in his usual hurried tone. "I hear we're going to the beach," he said in his funny tongue-too-long-for-his mouth voice. I'd been waiting to mention it to Shimada until after Yoko agreed, and I couldn't imagine that Yoko herself would have mentioned it to him. I could only conclude that Akira must have spilled the beans. It was all the same to Shimada.

"I'm free to go. Any time. I've been thinking of quitting. For a while now, actually. My job, I mean. I already got my bonus. So the timing's perfect."

This was pretty big news for such an off-the-cuff announcement. "What will you do if you quit your job?" I asked.

"I'm thinking of writing a novel," Shimada replied. From the look on his face it was clear that he didn't think there was anything unusual or outrageous in what he had said.

I found myself going along with him. Shimada's relaxed approach could be contagious. But couldn't he write a novel without quitting his job?

"I don't think so. That wouldn't work for me. When I'm at work I give it my all. It tires you out, working the way I do. And besides, they always find things for you to do, right? I've put in two years with the company. I looked at my bank balance recently, and it turns out I have a fair bit saved up."

I wasn't entirely convinced by this line of argument, but Akira interrupted before I could say anything.

"You mean you have enough to keep you going for a while even if you don't work?" Akira turned to me with a smile. This didn't escape Yoko's notice. "You're pretty sharp today, Akira. You have no money, and you don't work. If other people want to do the same, what concern is it of yours?" She stood up and went into the kitchen to prepare the evening meal.

Akira seemed to get a real kick out of worrying about other people's money. Since he never had any himself, it would have been a waste of time for him to worry about his own finances—most of the time he would have had literally nothing to worry about. A more cynical (or more realistic) response might have been to suggest that Akira worried about other people's money only insofar as he relied on other people to look after him. But I don't either of these explanations was quite right. I think he reacted the way he did because he was more aware than most people realized of the fact that he needed money himself if he was ever going to learn to live his life without thrusting himself on other people's charity and moving from one friend's house to another.

I was quiet for a few moments, but I had to say something. "Why don't you just tell your boss you're quitting to write a novel?" The words came out of my mouth before I'd had time to think. Shimada looked at me as though he hadn't understood what I'd said. Gonta spoke up.

"It's funny how even adults have to play games with each other, isn't it?"

Now that he mentioned it I could see how what I'd suggested might be taken as a kind of strategy on Shimada's part to squeeze his boss for a raise. I was musing quietly about this to myself when Shimada spoke again.

"My boss is a *yakuza*." Oh really, I said—or words to that effect. Probably he'd mentioned it to suggest that you couldn't afford to play games when you were negotiating with gangsters. "Did I never mention it before? It's not like he's at the office all the time. He has some place of his own. He buys up golf courses and stuff." I didn't respond. Instead I reminded Shimada of something he'd told me recently—that he'd been praised at work as a man of rare abilities and promise. "Well, yeah. Actually, they seem to rate me higher than ever these days, for some reason."

"That's perfect. Maybe your boss will offer you a special deal. You can become a part-time employee, so that you only need to go into the office three days a week or something. You could use the rest of your time to write your novel."

"It's not going to happen." Shimada sighed and gave a wry smile. But for some reason I felt optimistic on his behalf; his superiors at work were sure to value him as an asset if he'd already been singled out for special praise—I tried to make my suggestion again, but really it was up to him to bring up the subject if he wanted to talk about it. And he obviously did not.

With Gonta there to give us an excuse, it was drinking rather than eating that became the focus of our activities around the dinner table that evening, although we did nibble on spaghetti as we sipped our beers. We carried on drinking once dinner was out of the way, some of us moving onto gin or whiskey, others sticking with beer. After a while, conversation turned to our trip to the beach. Where did we want to go?

"What do you mean? I thought we'd agreed we were going to the beach?" Akira said. Evidently it didn't matter much to him where we went, so long as there was sand and sea.

How about Shonan, I suggested. Great, said Akira. Or Nanki-Shirahama? Sure, let's go there. Akira was more desperate to go the beach than any of us but—as is often the way—he was no use at all when it came to deciding where we should go. But even if faraway places like Okinawa and Nanki-Shirahama were obviously out of the question, we still had a number of options to choose from: Izu or Shonan, or the Miura peninsula, or Katsuura or Kujukuri in Chiba. We went through each of the choices in turn, explaining a bit about them to Akira; Izu is known for its white sand, Kujukuri faces onto the open seas and has big waves, and so on.

Then someone pointed out that if we went to Izu or Katsuura we'd have to stay the night, whereas we could make it to somewhere in Kanagawa and back as a day trip. So first we had to make up our minds whether we were looking for a day trip or an overnight stay. Akira's vote didn't surprise anyone. "Let's stay the night." But Yoko said she'd prefer a day trip. She was pretty clear on the subject, actually. We were all a bit taken aback by this, but Akira wasn't ready to back down so easily.

"But it's way more fun if we stay the night," he said.

"I don't mind staying the night, but I just think we should go somewhere where we can cover the distance in a day trip," Yoko said—not so much to Akira as to all of us. Why was she so keen to stay within easy striking distance of Tokyo? All of us knew there could be only one reason. It was Akira, more desperate than any of us to get this settled as soon as possible, who came out with what we were all thinking. "Because of the cats?" he said. But Yoko just repeated what she'd already said. "Personally, I'd rather go somewhere where we get there and back in the same day." Everyone was silent. She went on.

"What if we go somewhere and I meet someone I really like? If that happens, I want to be able to go and see them again any time I want. If they lived far away, I'd probably never see them again."

Yoko didn't seem to have romance in mind. Her imaginary friend might just as well have been another girl or an old man with a pipe and a white beard for all it mattered. It almost made sense. Surprisingly enough, it was Shimada who spoke up with a canny counterargument.

"Sometimes it's nice to know that you've got someone special waiting for you in a place you can't get to visit very often," he said. He sounded like a big brother trying to talk sense into his little sister. He didn't sound like his usual self at all. Someone special? Even Gonta had to struggle not to giggle at the sound of that. But Shimada seemed to have expected nothing less and looked seriously into Yoko's eyes. "But it's not the same if you know you can't see that person again whenever you want," she said. This was the thinking that made Yoko go out every day to distribute alms to the neighborhood cats. There was something touching about it, I thought—and I said so. "Just like the way you feed the cats every day, right?" I said. Yoko gave me a smile of approval. "What, so you're going to feed this new friend every day as well?" Shimada said. He was in pretty good form.

Eventually, we agreed that we would go to a beach near Kamakura, and luckily enough when we called the hotel to make a reservation they still had rooms available. After that we were free to revert to our usual small talk. I wanted to know more about the thought process that had made Yoko change her mind since Akira had first started his obsession with the idea of going to the beach.

She had said she didn't want to go somewhere far away that she could visit only infrequently, an answer that stemmed from the same thinking that lay behind what she was doing with the cats at the time. It was almost as though she wanted to treat the trip as part of daily life rather than some kind of special occasion, and I wondered whether there was more to her attitude—some aspect of her thoughts that she hadn't put into words that evening or that perhaps she wasn't able to express. I wondered if she would ever be able to give expression to these feelings—perhaps that was exactly what she was already doing when she went out to leave food for the cats every day after all. And then I remembered Akira's pictures. Perhaps the thoughts that ran through Yoko's mind as she distributed the food were somehow reflected in Akira's photographs. I was possessed by an urge to see the pictures Akira had been taking of Yoko since they had moved in with me.

All of this made me feel like talking things over with Yumiko again. I called her after lunch the next day from a phone booth near Ebisu station. She picked up on the third ring.

"Hello, stranger. I'm just breast-feeding at the moment, actually." I had to laugh—this seemed an odd way to start a conversation over the phone with someone who didn't call more than once in a blue moon. But maybe she talked about this kind of thing with everybody.

"Don't be silly—you're not just anybody. But come to think of it, I wouldn't want to work with anyone unless I felt comfortable talking to them about this kind of thing, so maybe it comes to the same thing. Maybe I do talk about it with just about everyone— everyone I know, anyway." I had another question, though: how long was it normal to breast-feed a child for?

"I don't know. I mean, my kid has been eating normal food for ages now. But I decided to keep on breast-feeding till he's five."

"Wow."

"Didn't I mention it before?" Yumiko asked, as if it were the most normal thing in the world. "I think it's good to provide a child with a strong maternal presence for as long as possible. Don't they say it helps give a child a more optimistic outlook on life?"

"Who says so?"

"Ah, maybe I just made it up. Anyway, that's what I think."

I couldn't imagine any child of hers being troubled by a pessimistic or gloomy outlook.

"You can't be too optimistic about these things. The first few years are a crucial period in a person's life—I'm going to do whatever it takes to bring my child up right." I decided it was time to get down to business. I thought Yumiko might not know who I was talking about if I just mentioned the name Yoko out of the blue, but she hadn't forgotten. "The cat lover, right?" She listened with what sounded like interest to what I had to say, and once I'd filled her in on the basics of the situation, gave her diagnosis.

"There are so many stupid kids around today, but every now and then you come across someone like that who still knows what's what." My reply to this got off to a bad start when I found myself saying the words, "Back in our day."

"What am I talking about? But then—what else am I supposed to call it? But that's not what I meant. I hate those guys who are always going on about how things were 'Back in our day.' That's what I wanted to say."

Once I'd given Yumiko a good laugh by setting out my reasons for using such a hackneyed phrase, I felt able to continue with what I wanted to say.

People ten years or so younger than us—the generation born ten years or so after the end of the war, for whom the Tokyo Olympics, the Osaka Expo, and the Winter Olympics in Sapporo had been the events that punctuated the early stages of our lives, who had entered university at a time when the student movement was (depending on how you looked at it) either still going strong or already on its last legs—a generation generally dismissed as having produced no writers or worthwhile literature at all until Kenji Nakagami won the Akutagawa Prize, who were always being told that everything that happened was determined by the state of the country or the world at large; whose whole view of the world was influenced by this way of thinking, and who were incapable of thinking or speaking about the world in any other way—well, compared to us, the people who had come up a decade or more after us, I said, looked at things from a totally different perspective. I noticed as I heard myself speak that I was starting to sound just like the guys who are always droning on about how things were "back in our day," but I decided to plow on to the end, only to be rewarded by nothing more than a slightly dismissive remark from Yumiko.

"It's just like you to think like that. Listening to you talk really takes me back. Maybe that's why you and I haven't always been able to see eye-to-eye—maybe it's because I've never been able to think of things in that way." She paused for breath, and I went on. "I realize that now. Or maybe I realized it before, and just keep forgetting."

"I'm pretty sure I always said it wasn't right to obsess about the big problems in life—that that wasn't the way to think about things. But no one else around me thought like that."

"What about me? I always said the same thing."

"You were the only one."

"One is enough. Anyway, even if you did talk like that when you were in college, at least now it's in quotation marks. That's one thing that's changed, at least."

This was more like the usual Yumiko—an explanation that explained nothing. "Remember you used to write book reviews for that surfing magazine after graduation?" she said.

"You make it sound a lot more impressive than it really was. What about it?"

It was the kind of memory that might come back to me once or twice a year—the kind of memory I didn't recall unless I happened to come across the words "surfing magazine" somewhere. I was surprised that Yumiko remembered it at all.

"You used to say it was a waste of time, that surfers don't read books. But that didn't stop you from doing your best to find books to write about. Books that even surfers might read."

I remember writing something about Haruki Murakami, only to be told by my editor that our readership wasn't interested in hard-to-read stuff like that. This was in the days before Murakami became a best seller. So I tried a piece about a novel by Yoshio Kataoka that had surfers as its main characters, but the response was the same: "They won't read this." I tried comic books and photo collections, but it was no good—my editor told me to concentrate on books you could imagine someone reading at the beach. I wrote articles about Australian surfing magazines and stuff, and somehow managed to scrape together enough material to earn my twenty-thousand-yen fee or whatever it was each month. "It was fun watching you try to come up with something that people with no interest in books might read, without trying to force books on people. Even if the surfers probably didn't read any of your recommendations in the end."

"You can't force people to read if they don't want to."

"That's what I mean. But you might get your message across in the end if you keep plugging away at it."

"Things like that?" I thought for a moment. "Like compromising yourself, giving up your beliefs, you mean?"

"I mean 'things like that,'" Yumiko said. "I don't know what you're talking about when you go on like that. Anyway, it's not the 'things like that' that's important—it's the 'keep plugging away at it' part that really matters."

This must have been what appealed to her about Yoko, I thought.

"You mean on a daily basis, as part of your daily routine, right?"

"Whatever, dummy," Yumiko said, leaving a long pause for the meaning of her words to sink in. "Figure it out for yourself." She was right. But there wasn't much we could say to continue the topic now.

"It's so hot!" I said out loud. Sweat had dripped down from my hair onto my neck and was rolling down my chest and back.

"Are you outside somewhere?"

"Yeah. But that's not why I said it was hot. I just wanted to hear the sound of my own voice."

"Whatever, dummy. You sound fine to me."

"Good. Just checking. I always feel good in the summer." We chatted for a bit, and I suddenly remembered about Ishigami.

"Apparently Ishigami's going to England next week."

"Wow, me too. Maybe I'll see him there."

"Japanese people are becoming much more international and cosmopolitan these days," I said. Even as I said it I realized that I was spouting again.

"Whatever. It's just that the yen's worth more nowadays," Yumiko said. "I don't see what's so cosmopolitan or international about people who go out of their way to meet other Japanese people when they're overseas," Yumiko went on. "We don't care about anything that's going on in the world—Chernobyl, the IRA, whatever—we don't care, we just go," she said with a laugh. She was starting to sound like Ishigami. And what was it with that laugh of hers anyway?

I was finding it difficult to keep up my side of the conversation. "What would Yoko think if she could hear us now, I wonder?" Yumiko asked. And with that, our conversation came to an end.

I don't often find myself longing to go traveling, but I could see how it might be fun if you had Yoko's approach to things.

But perhaps the significance of traveling to distant places hadn't yet dawned on Yoko. Maybe she'd feel differently about things in the future.

That night turned out to be a continuation of the night before, and Akira, Yoko, and Gonta all kept on drinking before crashing out around midnight. Shimada, though, was out late, eventually turning up outside the apartment in a taxi around two in the morning.

There was a strong whiff of booze on his breath, but he looked quite sober; he sat down without taking off his suit or even loosening his tie and picked up the conversation we'd been having the night before.

"So I talked to him today—my *yakuza* boss. He thought about it for a bit and then told me to come out for a drink with him. He took me to some club."

I knew that Shimada wasn't going to treat me to any stories about the hostesses. "Then he says to me, 'Why don't you write my biography?'"

I couldn't make out if he was being serious. "His biography?" I said "Wow, so these things really do happen." I was impressed, but I couldn't help laughing too.

"So you believe it?" Shimada said as he took off his suit jacket.

"Sure. I mean, obviously."

"All right."

He remained silent just long enough for me to grow suspicious. Was he just putting me on after all? But Shimada wasn't like Akira, and I knew that this pause was not just for theatrical effect. He was making a note to himself that there really were people who would believe what he said without question.

"I didn't believe it myself," he said. "Not at first. But what can you do? So I was sitting there drinking whiskey and water and wondering what to say. And the girls there—the hostesses? They must all be younger than me, but they seem so grown-up. And they're always sitting there mixing you drinks. It's hard to relax. Then the boss comes back at me again with the same thing. *Come on, how about it? Will you write it for me or not?*"

"He must be for real then."

"I guess. Do you think I can take him at his word, though?" he asked, tugging his tie slowly from his collar. He had a strange look on his face.

"What do you mean? Is he in the habit of telling lies, this *yakuza* boss of yours?"

Shimada laughed. "No. Not as far as I know."

"Then he must be serious."

"I suppose you're right." Shimada was slowly coming to terms with it. "But he's a funny old codger." Suddenly I wasn't sure who he was talking about.

"You mean your *yakuza* boss?"

"Right."

"Is that how people talk about the *yakuza* these days—funny old codgers?"

"I don't know. But that's just what he's like." This didn't tell me much. I needed concrete examples. "Like the kind of guy you might find coaching a little league baseball team?"

"No, that makes him sound like a grocery store manager."

"Like a gorilla keeper at a zoo?"

"No, he's not like any of those at all," Shimada said. He mused silently for a few moments before he put his finger on it. "I know," he said. "Godard. That's it. Godard. Imagine a slightly less skinny version of Jean-Luc Godard—just a bit more meat on him. Internally as well as externally. Oh, I don't know—something like that."

"Kind of intellectual-looking? Something suspicious about him?"

"Something like that. Not suspicious, exactly—just not entirely genuine."

Now it was my turn to have my doubts about the boss's offer. How could you trust a man who smelled of bullshit? But what Shimada seemed to mean was that there was something unreal about his boss; that he didn't seem to fit into any of the normal categories.

"How do you mean?" I asked. Shimada thought it over for a few seconds, and then started to speak in a voice quite different from his usual voice. Was he imitating the way his boss spoke?

"'People shouldn't do things they're not cut out for. If you do, the effects make themselves known on your body. You get too fat or too thin. Your complexion gets bad. Look at me: I've never done anything but what I was cut out to do. That's why my face is so smooth today.'

"He does turn up at the office from time to time, though. We all sit there working away with serious expressions on our faces. And he comes up with shit like that. It's funny, right? I mean, what kind of message is that to give your employees?

That's what I mean—there's something unreal about him. The way he lives his whole life is just unbelievable to me."

He kept on about his boss until we were in danger of losing sight of the topic at hand. Suddenly Shimada got serious. "I don't know. Maybe I should just say no." Every word was like a sigh. I did want to hear more about his boss, so I muttered something noncommittal and thought about what I should say to Shimada, but after a while it just didn't seem worth the effort.

"What about money?" I said, changing the subject. Knowing Shimada, I suspected that money wouldn't have been discussed at all. I was only half right.

"Money? Well . . ." he looked less sure of himself than ever. "It came up. I mean, he told me about it. Look, he's a *yakuza*." There was a serious look on his face for a few moments as he struggled to remember the details. He shook his head and looked up at the ceiling.

"Ten million yen? No, wait a minute—maybe it was just one million. No, it was more than that. I guess it must have been ten million. Yeah, that sounds about right. I can remember I was pretty surprised by how much he was offering," Shimada said, nodding to himself. But then his face clouded over again.

"But there were all kinds of conditions. So much if I don't do a good job. So much again if things go well and the book is sold in regular bookstores. And so on. But I don't know if I should even accept the job. I mean, I wasn't even listening properly." This was pretty typical.

No matter how much he might refer to him as a funny old codger or a fishy old man who looked like Godard, though, this was not the landlord of some broken-down apartment building we were talking about, but a real-life gangster. The fact that he could sit face-to-face with a mobster and still not listen to what he was saying should give you some idea of where Shimada's head was at. I suppose you could call it a kind of bravery. Maybe his boss had misinterpreted this as a sign of special promise, and that was why he had come up with the idea of asking him to write his biography.

We talked for a bit more about his *yakuza* boss; whether he would write the man's biography or not was still up in the air. But one thing was certain: Shimada would no longer have to go to work every day as he had done till now. He had the very next day off.

"You want another drink then?" I asked. Akira and Gonta got up again too and started on the gin. After a while Yoko woke up and joined us, and we ended up drinking together till four in the morning.

5

We set off for the beach in a rental car at five o'clock the following Tuesday morning, Gonta at the wheel.

Akira plunked himself down next the driver despite the fact that he didn't know how to drive, treating us all to several renditions of his early-morning songs and blasting his own mix tapes over the stereo—everything from girl bands to reggae and punk rock. Anything—so long as it was loud and impossible to ignore. But by now we were all used to Akira's noise, and the three of us in the back seat spent most of our time dozing, so that after a while Akira's noise-making activities were aimed solely at Gonta. But Gonta had built up a fair amount of immunity to Akira's antics by now, and we arrived on schedule around seven.

There is a special feel to the day at seven in the morning. It wasn't warm at all, and I was slightly worried that the day would never get as hot as it had been the day before. After several weeks of bright sunshine, it would be just our luck if it clouded over now that we'd finally made it to the coast. But the cool freshness typical of a summer's morning was a revelation only to a late riser like me. Everyone else seemed to know it was nothing to worry about.

Another surprise was how deserted it was everywhere. We were practically the only people on the whole beach. We didn't have the place entirely to ourselves, though: huge squadrons of crows were picking at rubbish and cruising along the shoreline in sky-darkening groups. Dozens of birds flew overhead at irregular intervals, cawing menacingly as they flapped their way through the sky above the waves and sand. It was such a strange sight that it took me a few minutes to get to used to it—once I did, I noticed for the first time the rising and falling heads of a group of surfers already on the waves. They bobbed patiently up and down for minutes at a time waiting for a wave; when one came the surfers would rise up en masse from the water and come surging in toward the shoreline, before turning around and paddling back out to sea again. I wandered slowly along the beach as I watched them.

We spread out a large sheet on the sand twenty or thirty meters from the shoreline and about the same distance again from the beach huts and set down our bags. We stood looking out to sea or up at the crows in the sky, but for some reason we were all slightly restless. Akira seemed unusually subdued, and although Gonta had his video camera on as usual, he wasn't filming with anything like his usual enthusiasm, while Shimada wasn't anything like his usual relaxed laidback self. Something had to be done, and I decided that I would do my bit by changing into my swimming trunks.

Unfortunately, the beach huts weren't open yet. This didn't make much difference to us guys—especially as there was nobody on the beach, I just wrapped a towel around my waist while I wriggled into my trunks. I was wondering how Yoko would deal with the situation when she stood up and slung her bag over her shoulder. "I'll get changed over there," she said, and slunk off toward the public toilets next to the beach huts. A little while later she emerged again with a T-shirt on over her bathing suit. We all watched at her as she approached, struck anew by how slim and attractive she was as she came into view. "I wouldn't be ashamed to be seen with you anywhere looking like that," I said. Akira was making embarrassed-sounding noises at my side—but he could hardly talk. Things were worse than ever now that we had changed into our swimming trunks. For a while we looked at each other awkwardly and started a few half-hearted conversations that faded into nothing before they'd even started. Akira stared at Shimada's emaciated body and suddenly burst out laughing. "You look like an old man!" he said. Shimada pulled on a T-shirt to hide his body. If that's the way you're going to be about it, he seemed to say. Seeing him with his T-shirt on caused the scales to fall from our eyes. We all hurried to get back into our own T-shirts.

Yoko looked at us as though we were babies. "Anyone would think you'd never been to the beach before," she laughed. What with the dizziness I was feeling on account of the early hour, and the excitement we all felt at the idea of being at the beach (an excitement that had Akira at its center, it has to be said), whatever anyone did or said seemed interesting and fun.

But everything at the beach really does look and feel different early in the morning. The feel of the sun and the breeze on my face changed gradually as the hours passed. I was surprised at one stage to notice a group of old people sitting formally with their hands joined in front of them on the sand, facing out in the direction of the sea and the sun. After a while, people started to come out in ones and twos from the houses that lined the shore—the rattle and clack of people lifting the bamboo blinds on the windows of their houses seemed to signal that at last our day at the beach was about to start in earnest. Early-morning dog-walkers began to appear up and down the beach.

One man in particular stood out from the rest. His voice could be heard loud and clear from far across the sands as he walked, although at first I couldn't make out whether he was talking to himself or his dog. I watched him come closer, and after a while my doubts were answered.

"Not so many surfers out today," he said to his dog. "There's not much wind, you see, so the waves probably aren't very good. Even the roar of the waves isn't as loud as usual. Can you hear that, Johnny?

"Look at those three crows over there by the trash cans. They're looking for something to eat in all that rubbish.

"Oh dear. Some other doggie's left his poop on the beach. That's not nice. Let's bury it in the sand so that no one steps in it.

"Look how much seaweed there is. Look, Johnny, this is called seaweed. The sea must have been pretty rough last night to wash all this onto the shore."

He hardly let up at all, nattering away to his dog as he walked past. He sounded like a father talking to his child. Once he was gone, Yoko looked at me with raised eyebrows. "Did you see that?"

"What was that all about?" I said. I looked over at Gonta, and realized that he'd had his video camera running the whole time.

"This is great," he said. "Ever since we got here, everyone's been looking around and studying their new surroundings. It's perfect material for my film." Apparently he had nothing to say about the strange man and his dog who had just gone past. As always, Gonta was more interested in capturing our reactions to things than in filming whatever it was we were looking at. He had kept his camera on Yoko and me the whole time as we watched the man walk by, but hadn't bothered to shoot so much as a single frame of the man himself.

After a while we started to settle into our usual rhythms; Shimada was stretched out on the edge of the sheet and well on his way to sleep. Shimada fell asleep at the drop of a hat wherever he was. Akira was the only one of the group who was not his usual self. No longer the loud and boisterous nuisance he had been all the way in the car, he was sitting contemplatively on his own and staring out to sea.

He had already calmed down by the time we arrived, I had noticed, and his reaction when Yoko reappeared in her swimsuit was far from the over-the-top reaction you would normally have expected from him. His eyes flitted back and forth from the surfers surging in on the waves to the windsurfers drifting across the horizon, occasionally looking up at the seabirds that flew overhead, before moving back to the shoreline and the waves, breaking off from time to time to look over at us. Yoko had noticed this too, and thought it as odd as I did.

"Aki-ra," she said, putting the emphasis on the last syllable of his name.

"Huh?" Instead of the theatrical laugh we were used to from him, Akira turned and smiled sweetly at Yoko.

"What are you doing?" Yoko said.

Apart from Gonta and his incessant video recording, none of us were really "doing" anything, and even Gonta's filming probably didn't really count as actually doing something either—all of us were basically "doing" nothing at all—but Yoko, like me, obviously felt that things weren't quite right with Akira sitting in silence like this.

"Nothing much," Akira said with a smile before turning to look back out at the sea again.

I started to feel sleepy too and was just drifting off when Yoko stood up and said, "I'm going to go grab a hamburger." I asked her to get me a beer and was just handing over my wallet when Akira got to his feet and announced that he would go with her. Gonta said that he would go too, and stood up with his video camera. The three of them walked off with Yoko leading the way. "You don't mind if we take our time, do you?" Akira called out in parting, in a voice that was surprisingly bashful for him.

I fell asleep almost immediately. The next thing I knew, they were standing next to me again and a hamburger and a can of beer were waiting on the sand about ten centimeters from my face. When I opened my eyes the sun was high in the sky and blazing down on us; I propped myself up with an elbow and looked around; everywhere I looked the beach was covered with people. It really felt like we were at the seaside now.

"Have you two been sleeping all this time?" Akira said. His voice had none of the whining quality it normally had, and I found myself muttering "yeah" without thinking. "Yeah?" Akira laughed. "It's such a waste to spend the whole time sleeping," he said, handing me a beer.

"Thanks," I said, and cracked the top open. "But that's what being at the beach is all about, you see. Eat a burger, have a couple of beers, take a snooze. Wake up, drink another beer. That's the whole point."

"Hmm, maybe," Akira said seriously, peeling the wrapper from the hamburger and devouring half of it. He stood looking out to sea, his jaw moving up and down as he chewed his burger.

"This is the first time Akira's ever been to the beach," Yoko said—half to herself, half to me. "It's not my first time—I never said that," Akira said. This too was said in a much more straightforward and normal tone of voice than we were used to from him. He immediately turned his back on us again and went back to staring out to sea.

"That's why he's so happy," Yoko said, but he didn't seem to hear her. Now that Yoko mentioned it, I realized why Akira's behavior was so different from usual, and I thought back on the way he'd been since we arrived at the beach. I watched him as he stood with his back to me, staring out at sea, and felt the happiness and contentment rising from him. Just looking at him was enough to make me feel content.

Our time at the beach passed slowly and happily—none of us did anything, but we were never bored. I did little more than drink beer and fall asleep; Shimada slept even more than I did; Gonta spent his time filming the rest of us and the scenery around us, while Akira either sat staring out to sea or went off for walks along the beach with Yoko. Akira gave off a strange sense of well-being, and Yoko seemed to float in a world of her own, not really seeming to belong to the group at all.

I woke up from one of my naps in the early afternoon to find Gonta alone by my side with his video recorder. There was no sign of any of the others.

"What happened to everyone?" I asked.

"Akira and Yoko went for a walk somewhere, and Shimada said he was going to go for a swim."

"So Shimada swims too, huh?" I wouldn't have pegged Shimada for a swimmer. "Have you been filming this whole time?" Yet another meaningless question escaped my lips.

"I've shot quite a bit. But I'm starting to feel like maybe I've done enough for today." Since he continued to film with his camera even as he said this, I wasn't convinced.

"I bet you won't stop," I said and looked over at Gonta's camera.

"Most of the time when I'm filming I tend to do it on my own. There are days like today when I film the people around me, but that's only part of it." Gonta couldn't have sounded much more Gonta-like if he'd tried.

"The thing is, when we first got here, everyone felt a little—what? Awkward? You know—we hadn't settled into our new environment yet. That's what made me think I'd be able to get some good footage. Like I said before when that guy came past talking to himself? But after a while everyone settles back into their own rhythm and there's not as much to shoot. I mean, there's still plenty to shoot, but . . . you know what I mean."

"Right," I said. But my lips were moving on their own.

"I mean," Gonta said with a pinched smile, "That's how it seems to me, anyway," he said, the video recording on his camera as he spoke.

"I just hope some of this will come across when people watch it," he said, then fell silent, watching his surroundings through the viewfinder of his video camera.

"You're not really interested in filming incidents, are you? Or coming up with an interesting storyline?"

"How can I explain it? I never remember stories—details of the plot and stuff like that. When I watch a movie or read a book, I'm always thinking of something else. But I always wanted to write when I was in high school. Just like I want to make movies now. But plot and storylines don't interest me. Not like these movies and plays where they take some real-life murder case and make a drama out of it. That doesn't interest me at all. It's just dumb if you ask me.

"Don't you think it's kind of weird to take your inspiration from some random event? Like murders—normally things like that just don't happen. If you were determined to write about something shocking, why not write about a road accident or something?

"These Japanese directors, they're always going on about how we live our lives side by side with tragedy and evil. But look at the stuff they put out: What's so 'side by side with tragedy' about that? The characters in their movies aren't even normal people.

"I prefer to shoot what happens around me—real life, from my real perspective.

"I want to show people that the life we live has nothing to do with the stories you see in movies or novels, where everything is simplified and dramatic and exciting. Our lives are our stories."

I gave a few low murmurs of assent to show that I was listening. I enjoyed hearing him talk.

"But when I look back on what I've filmed, it's not so clear to me anymore what kind of world I'm living in. Most of the time I can't remember what was going through my mind when I shot the footage."

He continued to film as he spoke, and it occurred to me that he was more interested in recording what he was saying than in capturing anything in particular on film—but this was Gonta, and he may well have had other motives that I knew nothing about.

"I showed some of it to Akira once. He said he thought it was pretty interesting." And then, speaking more clearly than usual, he said: "The great thing about Akira is that he doesn't have any fixed ideas about what a movie should look like." It was unusual for Gonta to come out with a definite statement like this. "For Akira, rules and definitions don't exist. I don't think he would even know what the words mean." He laughed then paused for a few moments before continuing.

"Like I said, I started out wanting to write a novel. But you can't write a novel where nothing happens. You can't just depict the simple passage of time in writing.

"But with moving images, if you just let the film roll and don't say anything, then there it is: time passing before your eyes. You can only really do it with video. It doesn't work the same with film, even though the images you capture might be the same.

"Like with those guys, you know," he said, lowering his voice.

For a while we'd been overhearing fragments of a conversation about mosquito nets from the neighboring group.

"Jumping on top of the net when the parents were trying to put it up, and getting an earful from the old man."

"Right, or getting it from his mother for lying in bed in the morning. 'Are you planning to stay in bed all day?!' she screams, and rips the netting down."

"And fumbling around in the dark trying to figure out whether you're inside or outside the thing. Whatever. Most of that's just bullshit. At least they can make up stories." I laughed under my breath. After a while we saw Shimada emerging from the sea and walking back in our direction. We waited in silence for him to reach us. He stood in front of us with heaving shoulders and a slightly breathless laugh.

"It's been a while. I'd forgotten how much hard work swimming in the sea can be," he said, collapsing on the sand without even bothering to towel himself off.

Gonta stopped filming and watched him. "Is that a general policy of yours?" he asked of Shimada, who had just lain down on the sand.

"What do you mean?" he said, not appearing to notice the sand that was sticking to his wet body. Shimada didn't act the way he did out of policy; he just was the way he was, and acted the same way wherever he went.

He was back on his feet almost immediately, sand all over his back. "I'm going to grab a beer," he said.

"Actually, Akira went off a while back saying he was going to bring back a few beers and some noodles," Gonta said.

Shimada's expression seemed to say, *In that case* . . . and he lay flat out on his back again in the sand. His arms were covered in sand, and he had piles of the stuff on his chest and belly; this didn't seem to bother him, though, and he was just drifting off again when Akira and Yoko reappeared with our beers.

"Have you been swimming?" Yoko asked. "You're covered in sand." Shimada glanced at his arms and belly, but didn't bother to do anything about it.

We did nothing in particular until the sun started to sink in the sky. The day had passed neither too fast nor too slow. Yoko suggested that we hire a rubber dinghy and go out to sea, and we all stood up together for the first time since we'd arrived at the beach.

We hired a dinghy big enough to fit five people. The boat came with a pair of oars, but we decided it would be quicker to get in the water and push. We ran into the sea together, all five of us swimming at the side of the dinghy and tugging it out to sea. The beach soon looked far away. The three- or four-story building near our spot on the beach was the only thing that enabled us to recognize where we'd been sitting just moments earlier. We were surrounded by windsurfers and sailboats.

We let the boat bob on the waves and drift with the current as we watched the yachts and the sea birds go by and gazed up at the mountains of the Miura peninsula and the cliffs of Inamuragasaki that surrounded the bay.

"It's not so hot out here at sea."

"I know."

"It's much cooler. Because of all the water, I guess."

"It's still not exactly cool."

"It feels just right if you ask me."

"It's cool when the wind blows, though."

"It's really nice."

"Yeah, the beach is great."

"Where's the place we were sitting just now?"

"Over near that building, I think."

"What building?"

"That one with the green roof."

"What, that's a building?"

"Well, what else do you want to call it?"

"Wasn't it a bit further over?"

"Over there near the river somewhere, right?"

"What river? You mean over there?"

"That big one over there."

"Have we really drifted that far already?"

"The tide's flowing in this direction."

"Wow Yoko, you know your stuff."

"Whatever, everyone knows that."

"Not me. I would never have thought of that if you hadn't mentioned it."

"You mean we're being carried by the tidal currents?"

"That makes it sound like we're adrift or something."

"But that's what it is. That's what I was thinking too."

"Yeah, it must be the currents."

"You don't think it's just the wind?"

"Yeah, it's probably the wind."

"What is?"

"The reason we've drifted so far."

"I don't think the wind would carry us this far on its own. It's not like we're in a sailboat."

"Those must cost a fortune."

"Tell me about it. Those are serious boats, man."

"So how much is the cheapest sailboat you can buy? Half a million? That's a lot of money to leave lying around on the beach."

"Yeah, but you can't just walk up and steal a sailboat. It's not like swimming trunks."

"I love the beach."

"Yeah, it's nice."

"What's that place called where people keep their boats?"

"A harbor? A marina?"

"With those small ones, people just carry them on top of their cars."

"Really, you just put it on top of your car?"

"That's got to be a challenge, steering one of those things."

"It must be easier in a place like this, though, in a sheltered bay."

"Or there wouldn't be so many of them here."

"Yeah. Plenty of room."

"One of them came over to where everyone was swimming before by mistake."

"You're keeping an eagle eye on things, I see."

"Then there was an announcement from that tower over there. *Get away from this area, quick!*"

"Well you would panic too, if it was you."

"At least they don't run people over."

"I love the sea."

"It's pretty cool just floating here like this."

"The water's all shiny. Like diamonds."

"It's beautiful."

"Do you think there are any fish down there?"

"Probably not around here."

"There might be some in the rock pools."

"Are there rock pools here?"

"Probably not around here."

"Why bring it up then?"

"This is great."

"Akira's not himself today."

"It's being at the beach that does it."

"Yeah, 'cause it doesn't cost anything to get in."

"You mean some places you have to pay?"

"That's not what I meant."

"Good."

"But even if there were, then we could still go to the free places."

"It's better if it's free, the beach."

"It's a good thing we didn't go to a super-nice beach."

"If it was a really nice one, Akira, you'd probably faint."

"That would be pretty hilarious."

"As if I would."

"Hey, look—is that a jellyfish?"

"Probably just a plastic bag."

"I don't know—it's pretty far down."

"Could be."

"How would you measure that, anyway?"

"What, the depth?"

"What's the point? What difference would it make if you knew how deep it was?"

"You'd be pretty freaked out if you found out it was 200 meters deep down there."

"What difference does it make, as long as you're on the surface?"

"But the pressure and stuff . . ."

"Whatever. You can drown in ten meters of water just as easily as one hundred."

"Even five is enough."

"I don't know. I think I'd be OK if it was only five meters."

"You wouldn't."

"But really—how deep do you think it is?"

"I don't even care. Man, I love this beach."

"Is it really green?"

"What?"

"What—the sea?"

"I don't know—it looks more like sand color to me."

"It's floating in the water—look, just thin little grains of it."

"Oh, you're right—it's sand."

"Maybe it's greener further out."

"Over here it looks kind of moss-colored."

"What do you mean?"

"Like a kind of gray."

"That's just the way it is."

"Well, it's not like the sky is really blue either."

"Did you see that? Something jumped."

"Yeah, I saw it."

"Must have been a fish."

"There *are* fish around here then."

"Look, over there!"

"Oh yeah. It's only a small one, though."

"There were fishing boats over here before, right Yoko?"

"Yeah, we saw them when we went for a walk on the beach."

"And fishermen."

"Really?"

"Yeah—they were fishing out there somewhere."

"Well, there must be fish then."

"It feels nice when you're out in the sun like this."

"On your flesh you mean?"

"Skin. Don't say flesh."

"I feel all dry."

"I feel nice and smooth."

"You're starting to turn pink, Shimada."

"His flesh?"

"You're so pale."

"What, you mean his flesh?"

"Whatever."

"You're pretty dark, Gonta."

"What, his flesh?"

"Oh, shut up."

"You've really got some color, Yoko."

"Yeah, all that time walking around in the sun, I guess."

"Hey, Yoko—did anyone try to pick you up?"

"With you guys hanging around her the whole time? I don't think so."

"She was on her own for a while."

"Is that all it takes—a few minutes on your own and they start crowding around you?"

"I don't know—no one's ever tried to pick me up."

"Really?"

"What about Akira, then?"

"Is that what you call picking someone up?"

"Why not?"

"That was different."

"Really?"

"It wasn't like that at all."

"Really?"

"He just came up and started talking to me normally."

"What do you mean, normally?"

"Shouldn't we be getting back soon?"

"Do you really think there are jellyfish round here?"

"Probably."

"You see lots of them at the height of summer when the tide is high."

"Ha ha!"

"What's so funny?"

"Sounds like the kind of thing a precocious child might say. At the height of the summer, when the tide is high . . ."

"Oh, really?"

"Hey, how come you never hear about those electric jellyfish anymore?"

"I saw them in a movie once."

"What, electric jellyfish?"

"Yeah. Some kind of porno."

"They'll use anything in those things."

"You saw it?"

"I was in my first year at middle school when that one came out."

"Ha."

"What?"

"That's a long time ago."

"Hey, look—that guy's tipped over."

"Wow, I've never seen anyone capsize before."

"Let's go over and see what happens."

"I don't think we should."

"Look what he's doing now."

"Come on, it's none of our business."

"Did you see the look on his face when he went over?"

"No need to talk so loud."

"He can't hear us."

"I bet he can."

"Who cares, anyway?"

"Hey, do you think that guy picks up a lot of girls?"

"What do you mean?"

"He could go over in his sailboat to where some girl's swimming and shout out to her, 'Hey baby!'"

"No way."

"Too bad."

"Yeah, I wish he would."

"Look, he's back up again now."

"That was pretty easy."

"It'd be way harder if this thing went over."

"Why—you think we're going to capsize?"

"No."

"That would be pretty bad. It's seriously deep out here."

"Look, even if I deliberately rock the boat . . ."

"It still doesn't move."

"Yeah, we should be all right as long as no big waves come."

"Hey, what if someone suddenly came up and gave it a big shove from underneath, though. I bet you'd be pretty freaked out."

"Obviously."

"It could be a turtle or something."

"Whatever."

"What, you don't think they have turtles in the sea?"

"Not around here."

"Or it could be some weird old man poking at the bottom of the boat with a pole."

"Yeah, whatever. What kind of old man?"

"I don't know—just some weird old man."

"There's not a single cloud in the sky."

"I love being at the beach."

"It feels like we've been marooned or something, floating here like this."

"Where would we end up if we just kept on drifting like this?"

"Dunno. Oshima, probably."

"Oshima?"

"Yeah, right. You sound like a couple of kids who think they can float all the way to America in their little toy boat."

"Really?"

"Yes, really."

"All right, so where would we end up then?"

"I don't know."

"I bet it would be pretty far away, though, if we got carried by the tide."

"We'd be like that stuff that gets carried on the waves and then washes up on a beach somewhere, miles away. Flotsam."

"I thought the water would be dirtier than this."

"This is the way it is."

"What's the character for 'tide' anyway?"

"Shio—as in Asashio."

"Asashio—what's that?"

"He's a sumo wrestler."

"Can't you think of a better way of explaining it? Since we're 'at sea' and everything."

"It's written with the water radical—then the character for morning."

"Isn't there another character for it?"

"A simplified one, you mean?"

"The water radical, with the character for evening."

"So if you write the full character it's the morning, and the abbreviated version is the evening."

"Hey, that's pretty funny."

"Actually maybe that's not a simplified version of the other character after all."

"Hey look—a seagull!"

"I knew there must be some around here somewhere."

"Hey seagull, come over here!"

"Maybe we should whistle at it?"

"It must be looking for fish."

"Yeah, it probably saw that one that jumped just now."

"Come on, let's get back to shore."

Two whole days went by like this.

After about four in the afternoon on the second day, the swimmers and day-trippers started to go home, and around five there was an announcement over the loudspeakers that the lifeguards were going off duty. Surfers and windsurfers began to appear on the marked-off area of the beach that been reserved for swimmers and families until now.

Our group remained hesitant to make a move. Occasionally one of us started to pack his things together, but no one else made a move to follow, and before long we were all standing staring vacantly out to sea again. Akira would start taking pictures, and Shimada would stretch himself out for a snooze on the sheet again—we all had our own ways of putting off the moment when we would have to get ready to go home. More and more people were out with their dogs now, and as we followed them up the beach with our gaze, we noticed the man we had seen talking to his dog the previous morning. This was our third sighting of him now, but this was the first time that all of us had been together and concentrating on him as he approached.

We could hear his voice quite clearly as he chatted to the dog while they walked along the shoreline, a good thirty meters from where we were standing.

"Look at that. We call this a shark. This one was probably still a baby. Look how small it is. Maybe some species are this small even when they're grown up, I'm not sure.

"But you're stronger than a shark, Johnny. Remember when that other dog came up and barked at us before? He soon changed his tune when you turned around to face him, Johnny.

"You're strong but kind, Johnny. Strong but kind."

The dog walked slowly by his side, keeping step. "That dog looks sad," Shimada said to no one in particular.

Suddenly, Yoko ran off in the dog's direction. We watched as she reached the shoreline and exchanged a few words with the man, but we couldn't catch a thing they were saying. I realized that the man must have been practically shouting until now.

No normal person goes around talking to himself in such a loud voice, I thought. Akira stood up and with a glance in my direction set off after Yoko. Perhaps he was thinking the same thing as I was—or maybe he was just following Yoko wherever she went. He was soon talking to the man too, and after a while Shimada and Gonta and I all set off to join them.

As we drew closer the man gave us a little bow and greeted us in a normal voice. "Apparently his dog's hard of hearing," Yoko said. I didn't understand what she meant.

Yoko must have heard it directly from the man himself. Either that or she had figured it out for herself from the way he was talking—but personally, I didn't know how seriously I was supposed to interpret the news. That the dog was slightly deaf didn't seem to be a satisfactory explanation at all for the way the man had been talking to it in such a loud voice. I didn't know what to say, so I just stood there with a dumb smile on my face. The man seemed to realize the inadequacy of Yoko's explanation and turned to speak to me in a subdued and hesitant voice.

"Think of it as rehabilitation, if you like. They say it can help old people who are going senile. Probably I shouldn't say things like that about him as his owner, but that's what it boils down to."

He paused for a moment and looked Shimada and me carefully in the face.

"But I'm not explaining this very well," he said with a laugh. At least he realized it.

"I've had this dog since I was in high school," he said. "He's seventeen now. That's old for a dog. When I was in college I used to commute from Kamakura. I didn't actually go onto campus that often, so things worked out fine. But then since I graduated I've been living in Tokyo. And all that time, I've hardly been back home. I know it's not very far, but that's just the way it goes.

"Then last year, the dog started to have problems with his hearing. His eyesight's not very good either." He stopped and looked at us as if to make sure that we were taking him seriously.

"He's very fond of me really," he said. "That's one thing I'm sure of. I don't know whether you'll understand what I'm about to say, but . . . I thought maybe it was because I wasn't here anymore that John—that's the dog's name, John—I thought maybe John felt he as though there was nothing for him to look at or listen to anymore if I wasn't here. As if he'd lost the will to live or something." He paused again and smiled the way people do when they're not sure if anyone will believe what they're saying.

"Well, that's my theory anyway," he said. Having glanced at us again to make sure that it was safe to go on, he continued with his story.

"People look and listen because they need to. When I'm at home, the dog's always listening for my footsteps. But if there's no need for him to pay attention anymore, then what's the point in keeping his ears pricked up listening for a sound that never comes?

"It was in the spring when his hearing started to go, and his eyesight started to fail around the same time. So I made up my mind to come home and spend time with him every day.

"And when I did, his hearing and eyesight really did get better," he grinned. "I'm sure you did the right thing," Yoko said. "Don't you agree?" she said, turning to us for support. I was nodding seriously to myself already.

His story seemed to suggest that there had been some kind of improvement in the dog's hearing since the man started talking to it. Was there really any connection between the two? Some people would dismiss his theory as nonsense. Some stories are convincing right from the start—no one could fail to believe that they are true. Others are clearly not true, and are merely propped up by the framework of fiction. The only requirement in this case is that they should be interesting enough to hold the attention of an audience. But then there are stories like this one, which some people will believe and others will dismiss. It's not the facts of the matter that make them convincing (or not)—their significance springs from a kind of collaboration of the will between the person telling the story and the person listening. These are the stories I like best.

I started to like the man too. He looked so relaxed as he told us his story, even though he had stopped several times to make sure that we were still listening. After a while his dog started to whine.

"I'd better be going," the man said. "I think the dog's getting mad at me for ignoring him." He turned to his dog and spoke loud and clear again. "I'm sorry! Let's go on with our walk!" Raising his right hand to us, he started to walk off with his dog. Suddenly,

Yoko realized that she hadn't asked him for his address and phone number—she didn't have anything to write with. In the end she asked the man—whose name turned out to be Ito—to speak his address and details into Gonta's video camera.

Gonta drove again on the way home, but this time Akira sat in silence all the way, his eyes fixed straight ahead. Occasionally he leaned forward to change cassettes, and I heard him repeating to himself: "The beach is awesome."

Plainsong is KAZUSHI HOSAKA's debut novel. Aside from his well-known love of cats, as seen in *Plainsong*, he is also fond of *shogi* (Japanese chess) and has written a book analyzing one of the premier players of the game.

PAUL WARHAM grew up in Lancashire and moved to Japan before studying at Oxford University and Harvard. The translator of Satoshi Azuchi's *Supermarket* and Kenzo Kitakata's *The Cage*, he is currently based in Tokyo.

PETROS ABATZOGLOU, *What Does Mrs.
  Freeman Want?*
MICHAL AJVAZ, *The Golden Age.*
  The Other City.
PIERRE ALBERT-BIROT, *Grabinoulor.*
YUZ ALESHKOVSKY, *Kangaroo.*
FELIPE ALFAU, *Chromos.*
  Locos.
IVAN ÂNGELO, *The Celebration.*
  The Tower of Glass.
DAVID ANTIN, *Talking.*
ANTÓNIO LOBO ANTUNES,
  Knowledge of Hell.
ALAIN ARIAS-MISSON, *Theatre of Incest.*
IFTIKHAR ARIF AND WAQAS KHWAJA, EDS.,
  Modern Poetry of Pakistan.
JOHN ASHBERY AND JAMES SCHUYLER,
  A Nest of Ninnies.
GABRIELA AVIGUR-ROTEM, *Heatwave
  and Crazy Birds.*
HEIMRAD BÄCKER, *transcript.*
DJUNA BARNES, *Ladies Almanack.*
  Ryder.
JOHN BARTH, *LETTERS.*
  Sabbatical.
DONALD BARTHELME, *The King.*
  Paradise.
SVETISLAV BASARA, *Chinese Letter.*
RENÉ BELLETTO, *Dying.*
MARK BINELLI, *Sacco and Vanzetti
  Must Die!*
ANDREI BITOV, *Pushkin House.*
ANDREJ BLATNIK, *You Do Understand.*
LOUIS PAUL BOON, *Chapel Road.*
  My Little War.
  Summer in Termuren.
ROGER BOYLAN, *Killoyle.*
IGNÁCIO DE LOYOLA BRANDÃO,
  Anonymous Celebrity.
  The Good-Bye Angel.
  Teeth under the Sun.
  Zero.
BONNIE BREMSER,
  Troia: Mexican Memoirs.
CHRISTINE BROOKE-ROSE, *Amalgamemnon.*
BRIGID BROPHY, *In Transit.*
MEREDITH BROSNAN, *Mr. Dynamite.*
GERALD L. BRUNS, *Modern Poetry and
  the Idea of Language.*
EVGENY BUNIMOVICH AND J. KATES, EDS.,
  *Contemporary Russian Poetry:
  An Anthology.*
GABRIELLE BURTON, *Heartbreak Hotel.*
MICHEL BUTOR, *Degrees.*
  Mobile.
  Portrait of the Artist as a Young Ape.
G. CABRERA INFANTE, *Infante's Inferno.*
  Three Trapped Tigers.
JULIETA CAMPOS,
  The Fear of Losing Eurydice.
ANNE CARSON, *Eros the Bittersweet.*
ORLY CASTEL-BLOOM, *Dolly City.*
CAMILO JOSÉ CELA, *Christ versus Arizona.*
  The Family of Pascual Duarte.
  The Hive.
LOUIS-FERDINAND CÉLINE, *Castle to Castle.*
  Conversations with Professor Y.
  London Bridge.
  Normance.

North.
Rigadoon.
HUGO CHARTERIS, *The Tide Is Right.*
JEROME CHARYN, *The Tar Baby.*
ERIC CHEVILLARD, *Demolishing Nisard.*
MARC CHOLODENKO, *Mordechai Schamz.*
JOSHUA COHEN, *Witz.*
EMILY HOLMES COLEMAN, *The Shutter
  of Snow.*
ROBERT COOVER, *A Night at the Movies.*
STANLEY CRAWFORD, *Log of the S.S. The
  Mrs Unguentine.*
  Some Instructions to My Wife.
ROBERT CREELEY, *Collected Prose.*
RENÉ CREVEL, *Putting My Foot in It.*
RALPH CUSACK, *Cadenza.*
SUSAN DAITCH, *L.C.*
  Storytown.
NICHOLAS DELBANCO,
  The Count of Concord.
  Sherbrookes.
NIGEL DENNIS, *Cards of Identity.*
PETER DIMOCK, *A Short Rhetoric for
  Leaving the Family.*
ARIEL DORFMAN, *Konfidenz.*
COLEMAN DOWELL,
  The Houses of Children.
  Island People.
  Too Much Flesh and Jabez.
ARKADII DRAGOMOSHCHENKO, *Dust.*
RIKKI DUCORNET, *The Complete
  Butcher's Tales.*
  The Fountains of Neptune.
  The Jade Cabinet.
  The One Marvelous Thing.
  Phosphor in Dreamland.
  The Stain.
  The Word "Desire."
WILLIAM EASTLAKE, *The Bamboo Bed.*
  Castle Keep.
  Lyric of the Circle Heart.
JEAN ECHENOZ, *Chopin's Move.*
STANLEY ELKIN, *A Bad Man.*
  Boswell: A Modern Comedy.
  *Criers and Kibitzers, Kibitzers
  and Criers.*
  The Dick Gibson Show.
  The Franchiser.
  George Mills.
  The Living End.
  The MacGuffin.
  The Magic Kingdom.
  Mrs. Ted Bliss.
  The Rabbi of Lud.
  Van Gogh's Room at Arles.
ANNIE ERNAUX, *Cleaned Out.*
LAUREN FAIRBANKS, *Muzzle Thyself.*
  Sister Carrie.
LESLIE A. FIEDLER, *Love and Death in
  the American Novel.*
JUAN FILLOY, *Op Oloop.*
GUSTAVE FLAUBERT, *Bouvard and Pécuchet.*
KASS FLEISHER, *Talking out of School.*
FORD MADOX FORD,
  The March of Literature.
JON FOSSE, *Aliss at the Fire.*
  Melancholy.
MAX FRISCH, *I'm Not Stiller.*
  Man in the Holocene.

CARLOS FUENTES, *Christopher Unborn.*
Distant Relations.
Terra Nostra.
Where the Air Is Clear.
JANICE GALLOWAY, *Foreign Parts.*
The Trick Is to Keep Breathing.
WILLIAM H. GASS, *Cartesian Sonata and Other Novellas.*
Finding a Form.
A Temple of Texts.
The Tunnel.
Willie Masters' Lonesome Wife.
GÉRARD GAVARRY, *Hoppla! 1 2 3.*
Making a Novel.
ETIENNE GILSON,
The Arts of the Beautiful.
Forms and Substances in the Arts.
C. S. GISCOMBE, *Giscome Road.*
Here.
Prairie Style.
DOUGLAS GLOVER, *Bad News of the Heart.*
The Enamoured Knight.
WITOLD GOMBROWICZ,
A Kind of Testament.
KAREN ELIZABETH GORDON,
The Red Shoes.
GEORGI GOSPODINOV, *Natural Novel.*
JUAN GOYTISOLO, *Count Julian.*
Exiled from Almost Everywhere.
Juan the Landless.
Makbara.
Marks of Identity.
PATRICK GRAINVILLE, *The Cave of Heaven.*
HENRY GREEN, *Back.*
Blindness.
Concluding.
Doting.
Nothing.
JIŘÍ GRUŠA, *The Questionnaire.*
GABRIEL GUDDING,
Rhode Island Notebook.
MELA HARTWIG, *Am I a Redundant Human Being?*
JOHN HAWKES, *The Passion Artist.*
Whistlejacket.
ALEKSANDAR HEMON, ED.,
Best European Fiction.
AIDAN HIGGINS, *A Bestiary.*
Balcony of Europe.
Bornholm Night-Ferry.
Darkling Plain: Texts for the Air.
Flotsam and Jetsam.
Langrishe, Go Down.
Scenes from a Receding Past.
Windy Arbours.
KEIZO HINO, *Isle of Dreams.*
KAZUSHI HOSAKA, *Plainsong.*
ALDOUS HUXLEY, *Antic Hay.*
Crome Yellow.
Point Counter Point.
Those Barren Leaves.
Time Must Have a Stop.
NAOYUKI II, *The Shadow of a Blue Cat.*
MIKHAIL IOSSEL AND JEFF PARKER, EDS.,
Amerika: Russian Writers View the United States.
GERT JONKE, *The Distant Sound.*
Geometric Regional Novel.
Homage to Czerny.
The System of Vienna.

JACQUES JOUET, *Mountain R.*
Savage.
Upstaged.
CHARLES JULIET, *Conversations with Samuel Beckett and Bram van Velde.*
MIEKO KANAI, *The Word Book.*
YORAM KANIUK, *Life on Sandpaper.*
HUGH KENNER, *The Counterfeiters.*
Flaubert, Joyce and Beckett: The Stoic Comedians.
Joyce's Voices.
DANILO KIŠ, *Garden, Ashes.*
A Tomb for Boris Davidovich.
ANITA KONKKA, *A Fool's Paradise.*
GEORGE KONRÁD, *The City Builder.*
TADEUSZ KONWICKI, *A Minor Apocalypse.*
The Polish Complex.
MENIS KOUMANDAREAS, *Koula.*
ELAINE KRAF, *The Princess of 72nd Street.*
JIM KRUSOE, *Iceland.*
EWA KURYLUK, *Century 21.*
EMILIO LASCANO TEGUI, *On Elegance While Sleeping.*
ERIC LAURRENT, *Do Not Touch.*
HERVÉ LE TELLIER, *The Sextine Chapel.*
A Thousand Pearls (for a Thousand Pennies)
VIOLETTE LEDUC, *La Bâtarde.*
EDOUARD LEVÉ, *Suicide.*
SUZANNE JILL LEVINE, *The Subversive Scribe: Translating Latin American Fiction.*
DEBORAH LEVY, *Billy and Girl.*
Pillow Talk in Europe and Other Places.
JOSÉ LEZAMA LIMA, *Paradiso.*
ROSA LIKSOM, *Dark Paradise.*
OSMAN LINS, *Avalovara.*
The Queen of the Prisons of Greece.
ALF MAC LOCHLAINN,
The Corpus in the Library.
Out of Focus.
RON LOEWINSOHN, *Magnetic Field(s).*
MINA LOY, *Stories and Essays of Mina Loy.*
BRIAN LYNCH, *The Winner of Sorrow.*
D. KEITH MANO, *Take Five.*
MICHELINE AHARONIAN MARCOM,
The Mirror in the Well.
BEN MARCUS,
The Age of Wire and String.
WALLACE MARKFIELD,
Teitlebaum's Window.
To an Early Grave.
DAVID MARKSON, *Reader's Block.*
Springer's Progress.
Wittgenstein's Mistress.
CAROLE MASO, *AVA.*
LADISLAV MATEJKA AND KRYSTYNA POMORSKA, EDS.,
Readings in Russian Poetics: Formalist and Structuralist Views.
HARRY MATHEWS,
The Case of the Persevering Maltese: Collected Essays.
Cigarettes.
The Conversions.
The Human Country: New and Collected Stories.
The Journalist.

SELECTED DALKEY ARCHIVE PAPERBACKS

My Life in CIA.
Singular Pleasures.
The Sinking of the Odradek
  Stadium.
Tlooth.
20 Lines a Day.
JOSEPH MCELROY,
  Night Soul and Other Stories.
THOMAS MCGONIGLE,
  Going to Patchogue.
ROBERT L. MCLAUGHLIN, ED., *Innovations:*
  An Anthology of
    Modern & Contemporary Fiction.
ABDELWAHAB MEDDEB, *Talismano.*
HERMAN MELVILLE, *The Confidence-Man.*
AMANDA MICHALOPOULOU, *I'd Like.*
STEVEN MILLHAUSER,
  The Barnum Museum.
  In the Penny Arcade.
RALPH J. MILLS, JR.,
  Essays on Poetry.
MOMUS, *The Book of Jokes.*
CHRISTINE MONTALBETTI, *Western.*
OLIVE MOORE, *Spleen.*
NICHOLAS MOSLEY, *Accident.*
  Assassins.
  Catastrophe Practice.
  Children of Darkness and Light.
  Experience and Religion.
  God's Hazard.
  The Hesperides Tree.
  Hopeful Monsters.
  Imago Bird.
  Impossible Object.
  Inventing God.
  Judith.
  Look at the Dark.
  Natalie Natalia.
  Paradoxes of Peace.
  Serpent.
  Time at War.
  The Uses of Slime Mould:
    Essays of Four Decades.
WARREN MOTTE,
  Fables of the Novel: French Fiction
    since 1990.
  Fiction Now: The French Novel in
    the 21st Century.
  Oulipo: A Primer of Potential
    Literature.
YVES NAVARRE, *Our Share of Time.*
  Sweet Tooth.
DOROTHY NELSON, *In Night's City.*
  Tar and Feathers.
ESHKOL NEVO, *Homesick.*
WILFRIDO D. NOLLEDO, *But for the Lovers.*
FLANN O'BRIEN,
  At Swim-Two-Birds.
  At War.
  The Best of Myles.
  The Dalkey Archive.
  Further Cuttings.
  The Hard Life.
  The Poor Mouth.
  The Third Policeman.
CLAUDE OLLIER, *The Mise-en-Scène.*
  Wert and the Life Without End.
PATRIK OUŘEDNÍK, *Europeana.*
  The Opportune Moment, 1855.
BORIS PAHOR, *Necropolis.*

FERNANDO DEL PASO,
  News from the Empire.
  Palinuro of Mexico.
ROBERT PINGET, *The Inquisitory.*
  Mahu or The Material.
  Trio.
MANUEL PUIG,
  Betrayed by Rita Hayworth.
  The Buenos Aires Affair.
  Heartbreak Tango.
RAYMOND QUENEAU, *The Last Days.*
  Odile.
  Pierrot Mon Ami.
  Saint Glinglin.
ANN QUIN, *Berg.*
  Passages.
  Three.
  Tripticks.
ISHMAEL REED,
  The Free-Lance Pallbearers.
  The Last Days of Louisiana Red.
  Ishmael Reed: The Plays.
  Juice!
  Reckless Eyeballing.
  The Terrible Threes.
  The Terrible Twos.
  Yellow Back Radio Broke-Down.
JOÃO UBALDO RIBEIRO, *House of the*
    Fortunate Buddhas.
JEAN RICARDOU, *Place Names.*
RAINER MARIA RILKE, *The Notebooks of*
    Malte Laurids Brigge.
JULIÁN RÍOS, *The House of Ulysses.*
  Larva: A Midsummer Night's Babel.
  Poundemonium.
  Procession of Shadows.
AUGUSTO ROA BASTOS, *I the Supreme.*
DANIÈL ROBBERECHTS,
  Arriving in Avignon.
JEAN ROLIN, *The Explosion of the*
    Radiator Hose.
OLIVIER ROLIN, *Hotel Crystal.*
ALIX CLEO ROUBAUD, *Alix's Journal.*
JACQUES ROUBAUD, *The Form of a*
    City Changes Faster, Alas, Than
    the Human Heart.
  The Great Fire of London.
  Hortense in Exile.
  Hortense Is Abducted.
  The Loop.
  The Plurality of Worlds of Lewis.
  The Princess Hoppy.
  Some Thing Black.
LEON S. ROUDIEZ, *French Fiction Revisited.*
RAYMOND ROUSSEL, *Impressions of Africa.*
VEDRANA RUDAN, *Night.*
STIG SÆTERBAKKEN, *Siamese.*
LYDIE SALVAYRE, *The Company of Ghosts.*
  Everyday Life.
  The Lecture.
  Portrait of the Writer as a
    Domesticated Animal.
  The Power of Flies.
LUIS RAFAEL SÁNCHEZ,
  Macho Camacho's Beat.
SEVERO SARDUY, *Cobra & Maitreya.*
NATHALIE SARRAUTE,
  Do You Hear Them?
  Martereau.
  The Planetarium.

FOR A FULL LIST OF PUBLICATIONS, VISIT:
www.dalkeyarchive.com

SELECTED DALKEY ARCHIVE PAPERBACKS

ARNO SCHMIDT, *Collected Novellas.*
  Collected Stories.
  Nobodaddy's Children.
  Two Novels.
ASAF SCHURR, *Motti.*
CHRISTINE SCHUTT, *Nightwork.*
GAIL SCOTT, *My Paris.*
DAMION SEARLS, *What We Were Doing*
  and Where We Were Going.
JUNE AKERS SEESE,
  Is This What Other Women Feel Too?
  What Waiting Really Means.
BERNARD SHARE, *Inish.*
  Transit.
AURELIE SHEEHAN,
  Jack Kerouac Is Pregnant.
VIKTOR SHKLOVSKY, *Bowstring.*
  Knight's Move.
  A Sentimental Journey:
  Memoirs 1917–1922.
  Energy of Delusion: A Book on Plot.
  Literature and Cinematography.
  Theory of Prose.
  Third Factory.
  Zoo, or Letters Not about Love.
CLAUDE SIMON, *The Invitation.*
PIERRE SINIAC, *The Collaborators.*
JOSEF ŠKVORECKÝ, *The Engineer of*
  Human Souls.
GILBERT SORRENTINO,
  Aberration of Starlight.
  Blue Pastoral.
  Crystal Vision.
  Imaginative Qualities of Actual
  Things.
  Mulligan Stew.
  Pack of Lies.
  Red the Fiend.
  The Sky Changes.
  Something Said.
  Splendide-Hôtel.
  Steelwork.
  Under the Shadow.
W. M. SPACKMAN,
  The Complete Fiction.
ANDRZEJ STASIUK, *Fado.*
GERTRUDE STEIN,
  Lucy Church Amiably.
  The Making of Americans.
  A Novel of Thank You.
LARS SVENDSEN, *A Philosophy of Evil.*
PIOTR SZEWC, *Annihilation.*
GONÇALO M. TAVARES, *Jerusalem.*
  Learning to Pray in the Age of
  Technology.
LUCIAN DAN TEODOROVICI,
  Our Circus Presents . . .
STEFAN THEMERSON, *Hobson's Island.*
  The Mystery of the Sardine.
  Tom Harris.
JOHN TOOMEY, *Sleepwalker.*
JEAN-PHILIPPE TOUSSAINT,
  The Bathroom.
  Camera.
  Monsieur.
  Running Away.
  Self-Portrait Abroad.
  Television.
DUMITRU TSEPENEAG,
  Hotel Europa.

  The Necessary Marriage.
  Pigeon Post.
  Vain Art of the Fugue.
ESTHER TUSQUETS, *Stranded.*
DUBRAVKA UGRESIC,
  Lend Me Your Character.
  Thank You for Not Reading.
MATI UNT, *Brecht at Night.*
  Diary of a Blood Donor.
  Things in the Night.
ÁLVARO URIBE AND OLIVIA SEARS, EDS.,
  Best of Contemporary Mexican
  Fiction.
ELOY URROZ, *Friction.*
  The Obstacles.
LUISA VALENZUELA, *Dark Desires and*
  the Others.
  He Who Searches.
MARJA-LIISA VARTIO,
  The Parson's Widow.
PAUL VERHAEGHEN, *Omega Minor.*
BORIS VIAN, *Heartsnatcher.*
LLORENÇ VILLALONGA, *The Dolls' Room.*
ORNELA VORPSI, *The Country Where No*
  One Ever Dies.
AUSTRYN WAINHOUSE, *Hedyphagetica.*
PAUL WEST,
  Words for a Deaf Daughter & Gala.
CURTIS WHITE,
  America's Magic Mountain.
  The Idea of Home.
  Memories of My Father Watching TV.
  Monstrous Possibility: An Invitation
  to Literary Politics.
  Requiem.
DIANE WILLIAMS, *Excitability:*
  Selected Stories.
  Romancer Erector.
DOUGLAS WOOLF, *Wall to Wall.*
  Ya! & John-Juan.
JAY WRIGHT, *Polynomials and Pollen.*
  The Presentable Art of Reading
  Absence.
PHILIP WYLIE, *Generation of Vipers.*
MARGUERITE YOUNG, *Angel in the Forest.*
  Miss MacIntosh, My Darling.
REYOUNG, *Unbabbling.*
VLADO ŽABOT, *The Succubus.*
ZORAN ŽIVKOVIĆ, *Hidden Camera.*
LOUIS ZUKOFSKY, *Collected Fiction.*
SCOTT ZWIREN, *God Head.*

FOR A FULL LIST OF PUBLICATIONS, VISIT:
www.dalkeyarchive.com